DOCTOR DESIRE

S.L. STERLING

Doctor Desire

DOCTOR *Desire*

USA Today Bestselling Author

S.L. STERLING

Doctor Desire

Copyright © 2021 by S.L. Sterling

ISBN: 978-1-989566-28-2

Paperback ISBN: 978-1-989566-33-6

Editor: Brandi Aquino, Editing Done Write

Cover Design: Thunderstruck Cover Designs

1

BRIELLE

Late Summer 2017

My back arched off the mattress, every inch of my body on fire as Sawyer ran his fingers around each nipple before trailing down my stomach. His lips met my abdomen, and he traced my belly button with his tongue, sending chills through my body. He lowered himself down and gently spread my legs, placing a kiss on each inner thigh, gently biting each side before he moved to the inside of my knees. I could feel his rough hands gripping me, and I murmured something incoherent and bit the back of my hand as I lifted my ass off the mattress, practically begging him to place his mouth on me. He'd been at this for hours. Every part of my body was on fire, and I almost hit the ceiling when he finally sank his tongue into my soaked center. The instant his tongue ran over my clit, I let out a loud moan, arching my back even more than before. His hands left my ass, and I could feel his rough hands on both of my breasts. He pinched my nipples hard between his thumb and forefingers as he sucked my clit into his mouth, sending more shock waves through me.

"That's it, baby. Lose yourself," he whispered breathlessly as he ran his tongue over me once again.

My mind spun. The entire summer with him had been like this. I'd spent many nights in his bed and in his apartment, as he fulfilled every need in my body, needs I didn't even know I had at the age of twenty.

"Do you want more?"

"Yes," I cried as I held back my release.

He grabbed my legs and placed them on his shoulders, and then sunk himself into me. He held on to my legs as he pumped into me with deep thrusts, pulling out just before I climaxed. He quickly flipped me onto my stomach and pulled me back onto my hands and knees and buried himself deeply into me, fucking me roughly as he held on to my hips and pumped hard into me.

"Don't you come yet," he said, his jaw clenched, each word forced out with a breath.

I closed my eyes and enjoyed every deep thrust he delivered, fighting my body's want for release when I felt him reach around and rub my clit, only heightening the need for release. He slowed each thrust to match the rhythm of his fingers. I buried my face into the pillow and bit my hand, doing my best to mute my moans.

He trailed kisses over my back, and without warning, I felt myself tipping over the edge, my body trembling, my moans loud. Sawyer McKay was going to be the death of me.

"That's it, baby," he moaned as he gripped my hips tight, and I felt his cock throb inside of me as he let go as well.

I collapsed onto the mattress, my body unable to hold itself up any longer. I felt him get up off the bed, the light from the bathroom spilling into the darkened room. In a matter of minutes, I felt the mattress dip back down as he crawled back into the bed beside me. He gently scooped me into his arms and lay back against the messed pillows.

He should have been against the law for me. I'd crushed on Sawyer for years, and I never dreamt in a million years that this would be happening. That we'd be laying in one another's arms, sweaty and out of breath. I closed my eyes and curled into his side, praying he wouldn't let me go because, deep down inside, I knew he had ruined me for any other man. Yet, I knew that good-bye was coming.

"I'm going to miss this," I mumbled, breathing hard, wiping my eyes, and looking at him as he came into focus.

"Summer isn't over just yet, baby," he whispered, placing a kiss on the side of my neck. "We have lots of time."

I nodded, giggling as his scruff tickled me. He kissed my neck and moved to my ear before meeting my lips, kissing me gently.

"Brie, I have a question for you."

"What's that?"

"You haven't by chance missed your pill, have you?" I looked over my shoulder at him, his face taking on a serious look.

"No, why?" I asked frantically, searching my mind to see if I could remember looking at the packet this morning to see if I could recall if all the pills had been taken.

"I don't want you to panic, but the condom broke."

"That's the third one this week." I swallowed hard.

"Perhaps the box was defective." He shrugged and chuckled as he pulled me closer.

"Sawyer...It's not funny. I can't get pregnant."

"Relax, Brie, that's why I asked. As long as you haven't missed any pills, I am certain we will be fine."

"How do you know that?" I questioned, feeling the panic rise in me. If I got pregnant, our secret would be out. My best friend would hate me, and my mother would be furious.

"I'm a doctor. I know these things. Trust me." He winked and smiled.

It was always that sexy smile that pulled me down from panicking—that and those dimples. I relaxed back into his arms and blew out a breath. I looked up at the ceiling, still not sure how to digest the fact the condom had broken again. "You're a soon-to-be intern. You're not a doctor yet."

"Actually, I am. I've graduated medical school," he whispered, his breath on my neck, his scruff tickling me once again.

I closed my eyes as his lips connected with my skin. "I could always help you take your mind off everything. Perhaps call it a prescription of sorts, and you know you need to follow the doctor's orders." He chuckled as he pushed himself up on his elbows and met my lips. I could already feel his growing erection poking into me.

I looked up into his eyes and slowly lifted my head to meet his lips. His tongue forced my lips apart and washed through my mouth, as his hands travelled down between my legs, his fingers slowly rubbing me with small circles. It took him only mere seconds to make me forget all about the broken condom, and soon I was once again writhing on the mattress as he brought me to the brink.

2

BRIELLE

I COULD HEAR the murmur of guests out in the living room as they left, while I quietly set the book I'd been reading to Emma down on the table. She was sound asleep against me, and I did my best to pick her up without waking her. I lay her down in her bed, pulling the covers up around her, then made my way to the door, looking back at her sleeping face one more time before shutting the light off. I pulled the door closed behind me. Where had the time gone? It seemed like only yesterday that I looked down into her scrunched-up little face the day she was born and instantly fell in love with her.

I looked around the apartment at the mess in the living room and let out a breath. It had been an amazing day. Emma's fourth birthday party had been a success. My sister and her husband had brought their three kids over, and my brother and his wife had brought over their two. We'd had dinner, and when I presented Emma with her cake, we all sang Happy Birthday. Mom and Diane, my best friend, had both snapped a picture of the cake I had made at the same time Emma sank her little hands into the soft icing and shoved a fistful of cake into her mouth.

I laughed at the thought as I looked around at the mess of paper plates all over the living room table. I was about to grab them when I heard Mom's laugh coming from the kitchen, followed by Diane's. Ignoring the mess, I wandered into the kitchen to see them both sitting at my little kitchen table, a glass of wine in front of them.

"She go down okay?" Mom asked, patting the chair beside her as she grabbed the bottle of wine and filled my glass.

"Yeah, she was fighting, but eventually, she calmed down. Everyone left?"

"Yep, we ushered them out, so take a load off, would you?" Diane said, shoving the full glass over to the only empty chair.

"I can't. I need to get everything cleaned up. I have to be at the bakery tomorrow morning at five. If not, then orders will not get filled." I sank my hands into the hot water in the sink and began washing some glasses.

"Brielle, honey, come now, take a rest. You've been going all day." Mom came up behind me, forcing the cloth out of my hand and taking over at the sink. "Sit down."

"Mom, I'm fine."

"Brielle, don't argue with me. Go sit down. It's bad enough you've had to raise that child on your own. Now, it's time to learn to accept some help when it's given to you."

"Fine," I said, holding my hands up in defeat. "Knock yourself out."

Diane let out a laugh. "She never accepts help."

"Don't you start on me too!" I cried.

"It's true. I'm always offering to help."

"Trying to fix me up is not what I call helping," I said, sipping on my wine.

"Your daughter is impossible. I've been trying to fix her up with some doctors from work. Every single time I mention it, she turns me down. I honestly don't think she wants the help. I think she likes to suffer."

I looked over at Diane. "Way to sell me out. Besides, I've told you I don't have time for a relationship right now. I have Emma, and The Cooling Rack, and..."

"And needs, Brielle. You have needs." Diane

laughed. "You are twenty-five years old! You have needs."

My mother looked over at me with what appeared to be concerned. She didn't fool me though; it was always the same look, one of disappointment. She'd never let me forget I had made a mistake when I decided to raise Emma on my own. However, I hadn't exactly been honest with her. Instead of the truth, I'd told her that the father had been a one-night stand.

"Diane, I'm fine. Honestly. I have enough on my plate. I don't need some guy coming in here and making my life more of a mess."

Diane gave me a knowing look and shrugged. "Can't say I haven't tried."

"I'd never say that. Besides, I still have that date with Drew in a couple of weeks—the pediatrician. I didn't cancel like I wanted to."

"Good! I think you will really like him. I'm glad you agreed to that."

"What choice did you leave me? He stood right in front of me as you went through my phone, looking for an available date."

Mom looked at Diane, an amused smile on her face as Diane giggled. "All right, fine, perhaps I was a little pushy. Anyways, I have to get going. Early morning for me tomorrow as well." Diane finished her glass of wine before making her way to the door.

"Okay, well, thanks for coming. It meant a lot that you were here."

"I wouldn't miss it for the world. I love that little nut," Diane said, leaning in for a hug before grabbing her purse off the back of the chair. Then she stopped and hugged my mother before she made her way to the door.

"I, too, should get going," Mom said, drying her hands on the towel, all the dishes now washed. "However, before I go, I could help you clean up the garbage."

I turned and looked over my shoulder into the living room and shook my head. "I'll be fine. Honestly."

"All right, suit yourself, sweetie. You have a good night then."

"I will. I'll get this cleaned up and then get to bed."

"Make sure you do. You look exhausted," Mom said, kissing me on the cheek, then slipped into her coat and shoes.

As soon as I locked the door, I grabbed the garbage pail and quickly made a beeline for the living room. Within five minutes, I had all the plates, forks, and plastic cups in the trash, and I quickly straightened up the living room before grabbing my glass of wine and placing it on the end table. I then changed into my shorts and T-shirt.

Before sitting down, I went over to the hall closet and reached up for the blanket I had put away earlier. I gave it a tug, but it was stuck on something, so I tugged a little harder. My eyes went wide as I saw a shoebox come crashing down along with the blanket. I quickly stepped back and caught the box just before it hit the floor.

Once I had caught my breath, I looked down at the old pink shoe box. I smiled to myself as I looked down at the familiar stickers covering it. I had totally forgotten I had shoved that up there as I ran my fingers over the stickers.

I carried the box over to the couch and curled up under the fuzzy blanket, placing it on my lap. I took a sip of wine and carefully lifted the lid. There were some pictures on top of my sister, brother, and me on summer vacation the year before my brother got married. I pulled out an old concert ticket stub and smiled. I remembered the concert. It was the last one I'd been to before Emma was born.

I reached into the box and pulled out a little black book. I flipped it, my fingers running over the gold *Diary* written on the front. I flipped open the cover and a soft smile fell on my lips. Hearts were drawn in sparkly pink ink all over the inside the front cover.

I turned the page and leaned back against the couch cushions and began reading the first entry.

Two hours later, I sat gripping the diary. I reached for my glass, picking it up. I went to take a sip and noticed it was empty. I got up off the couch and walked to the kitchen, pouring myself another glass. "So much for an early night," I mumbled to myself, looking at the clock. It was already one.

I made my way back to the couch and sank down into the cushions, picking up the diary. The date October 2, 2017 was scrawled on the blank page. I flipped to the next page to notice it, too, was blank. Not that I had forgotten because I would remember that date forever.

I stood in my bedroom, looking out the front window. The bright-orange and yellow leaves danced in the sunlight as I looked at the clock. It was almost seven. I took one last look at myself in the mirror and smoothed my skirt. I was meeting Sawyer for dinner, but first I headed into the washroom and looked down at the pregnancy test I'd taken only a few minutes earlier. Two dark-pink lines looked back at me as I ran my fingers through my hair, panic filling me. I took a moment to gather my thoughts and figure out how I was going to tell him. We were only supposed to be having fun, nothing serious.

I grabbed the pregnancy test off the vanity, wrapped it up in tissues, and buried at the bottom of the garbage can, then I pulled the bag from the can and tied it closed. That was the last thing I needed my mother to find, I thought to myself as my thoughts ran rampant.

I ran down the stairs, yelling good-bye to my mother, and made my way out to the car, first dumping the bag into the garbage can that sat at the curb. I backed down the driveway, wondering how stupid I could have been. What had I been thinking, hooking up with my best friend's brother, mutually agreeing to be friends with benefits for his last summer at home. Just because we were both single didn't give us permission to screw around. We had been careful, but the last three times we had been together, the condom had broken, and I had somehow missed two birth control pills. I mentioned nothing to Sawyer about missing those pills and really tried not to give it much thought, until my period had been almost three weeks late.

Sawyer and I had a quiet dinner at one of the fancier restaurants on the other side of town. Tonight was our good-bye dinner. Sawyer had spent the summer applying for internships, and he had finally been accepted; however, the hospital was out of state. Sawyer leaned back against the chair and looked at me.

"It looks like something is weighing on that pretty little head of yours."

I shook my head. "No, just going to miss you is all. When are you're planning on leaving?"

"Monday. I wanted to tell you sooner, but I wanted to make sure that everything was solid first before telling you. You know that I had an apartment and everything."

"So, basically, we only have tonight?" I questioned.

"Unfortunately," he said, studying my eyes. "I know it's been hard on you to keep this from Diane, but I want to let you know that this summer was...amazing."

Keeping the fact I'd been sleeping with my best friend's brother quiet from the only person I ever talked to about my private life had been stressful. It was going to be even more stressful now, especially since she thought I had been single all this time. I couldn't hide the fact I was pregnant for very long, and I feared I would crack when she confronted me about it. She would want to know who the father was, and I knew that if she found out it was her brother she may never speak to me again.

I smiled. "It certainly was. I really can't believe that tonight is it. Our last night together." Our eyes locked as the words fell from my lips, and I shifted in my seat. I knew the look in his eye all too well. He was hungry...for me, as I was him.

"It doesn't have to be the end, Brielle. I mean, I will come home occasionally. Plus, you could always come visit me as well, especially if you need a break from school."

I thought for a moment. "I'm sure I could, but only if you would want that."

"Brielle, of course I want. I wouldn't suggest it if I didn't. I don't want to be away from you, but I haven't gotten a response from any other internships that I applied for. If only Eastport General had taken me, then we wouldn't have to be apart, but perhaps this being apart will allow us to explore the possibility of something more. Give us a chance to miss one another."

I swallowed hard. We hadn't talked about anything permanent, and with the information I had just found out, I wasn't sure I was ready to be talking about it either. It was in this moment I wished I could call Diane and ask her for her advice. However, after we had finished desert, that thought flew from my mind as I followed him back to his condo and spent the next three hours wrapped in his sheets.

Monday morning, his family drove him to the airport. I'd wanted to go with them but didn't think it was appropriate to interrupt the personal family time. Instead, I drove to the airport and parked on a side road and watched his plane take off from the front seat of my car, never getting another chance to say good-bye.

Once he landed, he called me to give me his address and number, and then we talked on the phone for a couple of hours. Over the first few weeks he'd been gone, I gave us a lot of the thought. I missed him something terrible, and that was when communication between us had shifted. He no longer spent nights on the phone with me; he was either working, sleeping or was just too tired. I knew he had been working hard, and I knew that the move had been a huge adjustment, but for some reason, those excuses weren't enough for me, but I, too, was going through a huge adjustment. My hormones were going crazy as his baby was growing inside of me—a baby he knew nothing of.

Mid-October, I'd started my first semester of Law School. I was out with my friends one Friday night, and as the conversation shifted to school, a realization came over me that there was no way I could complete even this semester with a baby on the way, never mind once she or he were born. The course load was already heavy, I was behind, and I was already exhausted. There would be no way I could keep up with all the case studies. I could barely keep my eyes open during my later afternoon classes. I cried all weekend over it, and the following Monday, I dropped out of school. My plan was to go to Seattle and tell Sawyer about the baby. It had been a long, emotional day, giving up my dream, but it got worse once I returned home and told my mother that I'd dropped out of school.

I'd never seen my mother look at me with such a mix of anger and disappointment before. She sat silently at first, staring off into space. Then the screaming began, and once she'd said all she had to say, I went to my bedroom where I lay in bed with tears streaming down my face, longing to feel Sawyer's arms around me. Once the tears stopped flowing, I got up and opened my laptop and booked my flight to Seattle.

I flew out three days later, finally feeling confident enough to tell him about the baby. I spent the entire flight going over what I was going to say in mind. I also imagined his response to the news and was actually excited about it by the time the plane had landed. I grabbed a cab and gave the driver Sawyers' address, and soon we were off making our way through the city.

I glanced down at my watch. It was almost four. I knew Sawyer was off early tonight, and I should arrive just as he got home. I watched out the window as the cab sped down the road, finally pulling to a stop outside of a three-story walk-up.

"Here you are, miss. That will be ten dollars."

I grabbed my purse, fishing through for my wallet,

and had just grabbed a bill when I saw Sawyer round the corner up ahead. My heart stopped; he wasn't alone. There, hanging onto his arm, was some brunette in scrubs. I continued watching them, my heart in my throat, as they talked and laughed. I could feel the tears burning.

"Miss, ten dollars."

My eyes blurred with tears as I continued watching them together. I swallowed hard and looked down at the money in my hand, and quickly shoved it back in my purse. "You know, silly me, I just realized that I forgot one of my bags at the airport." I swallowed hard, not taking my eyes off the two of them. "Could you take me back?" I questioned, meeting the driver's eyes.

"Sure thing, miss. Is everything okay?" he questioned.

I nodded, afraid if I said anything, I would break down in tears. I sat back in the seat, and as he pulled away from the curb, I looked back over my shoulder and watched as Sawyer and the brunette climbed the stairs to the door. He opened the door and placed his hand on the small of her back, allowing her to enter the building, just like he'd done with me so many times.

I'd been stupid to believe I was special. I closed my eyes and rested my hand on my lower abdomen and swallowed hard. I really had no right to be upset. We were friends with benefits and nothing more, and I had been stupid to think we were more than that. I rested my head against the seat and watched the buildings pass by, until we had pulled back up to the airport.

Three weeks after I'd returned, I'd finally broken down and told my mother the real reason for me dropping out of school. I was pregnant. She yelled at me for hours, at how irresponsible I'd been and that I'd ruined my life. Then she demanded to know who the father was. "Let me guess, it's Sawyer, isn't it?"

"What?"

"It's Sawyer, Diane's brother. You two spent a crazy amount of time together this summer."

"Mom, no, it's not Sawyer." Since no one really knew he and I had been sleeping together, I decided the only way to deal with this was to lie to her, and so I told one enormous lie.

"It's a guy I meant one night out with the girls, just a one-night stand. I don't even have his number." That only made her more furious.

I was not proud of the lies I'd told, but I felt at the time they were necessary. That night I'd made a call to Diane. I needed my best friend now more than I ever thought possible, and so I told her the same thing.

I LEANED MY HEAD BACK AGAINST THE COUCH CUSHIONS and took in a deep breath, and that was when I noticed I'd been crying. I wiped my cheeks. I hadn't spoken to Sawyer McKay since I'd gotten out of the cab. Still, to this day, no one knew he was the father. I remembered him calling me for weeks after I'd flown to Seattle. He left me messages, begging for me to return his calls, but I couldn't. Soon, the calls became fewer and fewer, and just like that, whatever our relationship had been had died.

Time passed, and eventually I had gotten over him, and Emma had been born. I now had this perfect little baby that soon became my world, and I was scared shitless. Eventually, I'd gone back to school and gotten my pastry chef degree, while Mom watched Emma. Then I'd opened The Cooling Rack and gotten myself into this apartment. I looked around at the furnished apartment and blew out a breath. Even though every year had been a struggle, I had done pretty well for us.

Suddenly, I heard Emma begin to fuss, and I threw the blanket off my lap and quietly entered her room. I gently pulled the blanket up over her and looked down at her. I was kidding myself if I said I never thought of Sawyer again because, looking down at Emma, she was the spitting image of him. I had a daily reminder of Sawyer every single time I looked down into her face. I missed him, and I'd have given anything to have another chance with him.

I blew out a breath, reached over and clicked off the lamp and turned on her little night-light, then walked to the door and pulled it half shut. I walked over and shut the lamp off beside the couch and wandered into my bedroom, setting the alarm for five and crawled into bed.

3

———

SWAYER

Five Weeks Earlier

"Hey, Sawyer."

"Brenda, good to see you."

"Think perhaps we could have a night cap tonight?" she asked, stepping up beside me and sliding her hand into mine as she continued walking with me toward my office.

"Ah, not tonight. Apartment hunting," I answered, stopping outside of the change room door and resting my arm on the doorframe over her head as she looked up into my face.

"Maybe another time, then," she whispered.

"Only if you promise to wear that sexy little number you had on the other night," I said in a low voice as I kissed her lips.

It was totally against hospital policy to fraternize with other staff members, but I'd become used to breaking that rule. In the five years I'd been here, I'd been with most of the nurses in the emergency department.

"I promise," she said between kisses. "Call you later."

"Sounds good," I murmured and leaned against the wall, watching her walk away from me. I waited until she disappeared down the hall and then made my way into my office. It had been a hell of a day. My body ached, and I was tired. It had started the second I had walked in this morning, like usual. I'd barely sat down when I was called immediately to the emergency room for a multi-vehicle accident, and just as we got that cleared, two life-threatening gunshot wounds had come in.

Once I was out of surgery, I'd made my way back to my office. I walked in, sat down, and took some time to continue my search to find some crappy, overpriced apartment. I'd found out two weeks ago that I was being kicked out of my current apartment thanks to my roommate's girlfriend. The pair of them had decided on a whim that she wanted to move in with

Mark and had told me over coffee and pancakes one morning. I'd quickly checked for any new listings and became frustrated at the fact I still couldn't find anything suitable. Then I turned to the pile of paperwork on my desk. I sifted through medical documents mixed with my mail when one envelope caught my eye. Instead of opening it, I packed up my bag, took the letter, and made my way to the doctors' lounge.

I'd just gotten out of a hot shower, wrapped a towel around my waist, and walked over to my locker. Reaching into my bag, I pulled the letter out of my bag and sat down on the bench. I looked over the envelope, my eyes darting to the Eastport General Hospital Logo in the top right-hand corner. Excitement filled me as I ripped the corner of the envelope.

I'd applied to Eastport General regarding an opening in their emergency department over three months ago. After not hearing from them, I'd figured they filled the position. I took a deep breath, ripped the envelope open, and pulled out the letter. Sitting back against the wall, I unfolded the letter looked down at the first words, 'Congratulations." That was the only word I needed to read. I had gotten the job.

I leaned back against the cool wall and blew out a breath. I'd been living in Seattle for almost five years, and I'd hated every single solitary moment of it. My parents were getting older and needed more help, and being this far away didn't allow me to help them as much as I'd like, but now I held my ticket back home in my hands.

I re-read the letter, looking down at the last paragraph. I had until today to respond. I quickly pulled my cell phone from my bag and dialed. As soon as I heard another voice on the end, I typed in the extension for a Dr. Ryan Richards.

"Hello, Dr. Richards."

"Yes, it's Dr. Sawyer McKay. I'm calling about the letter you sent me regarding the position open at Eastport General."

"Ah, yes. I was beginning to think I wouldn't be hearing from you and that I'd have to return to my applicant pile."

"Sorry about that. It's been a crazy few days. If you haven't already filled the position, I am looking forward to starting at Eastport General."

"Glad to hear it. Your resume speaks for itself. How long will it take you to get here?"

I tapped the corner of the letter quickly, going over in my mind all I'd need to do. "A month too long?"

"See you then. In the meantime, you have my number should you have questions. Let me know once you arrive in Eastport. I would love to give you a tour of the hospital."

"Sounds good."

I hung up the phone as excitement filled me. I was going home.

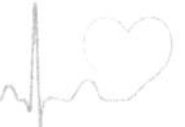

"I CAN'T BELIEVE YOU ARE FINALLY HOME," DIANE SAID, coming into the kitchen of our parents' home. I looked up from the paper I was reading and smiled.

"Hey, sis. How's things?" I said, getting up and hugging her.

"As well as I can be with an asshole of an ex-husband making my life a living hell, but let's not talk about him right now. So, my big brother is going to be working with me at Eastport. Everyone is so excited to have you there," she said, sitting down at the table across from me.

"So, I've heard. What about you? Are you excited to have me there?"

My sister and I hadn't always been on the best terms. She'd married an asshole, I'd tried to warn her, but she was determined to prove me wrong. My interfering had only made our relationship worse. She was now separated, but he still worked hard to make her life a living hell. I was just glad she was finally away from him, and now that I was back in Eastport, I was determined to try and have some sort of a relationship with her.

"Oh I guess. It will be an adjustment taking orders from my brother in the workplace." She laughed.

"No, it won't. You won't be working directly with me. I made sure I told them that we were related," I said, sitting back in the chair taking a drink of my water.

"Have you seen some of the old guys since you've been back in town?" Diane asked. "I know Lions asked about you the other day, and so did Paul."

"God, I haven't thought about those guys in a long time. Probably since the party they had back before I left for school. I sort of drifted apart from everyone when I left."

"Lord, don't remind me of that. That was the party I met Leo at. I thought he was so hot." She buried her face in her hands in embarrassment. "Little did I know what he would turn out to be," she said, screwing up her face in disgust.

"Yeah, well, had I of known you were running off with him when you did, I would have put a stop to it."

"You wouldn't have won. I mean, Brie did try and stop me, and I didn't listen to her either."

A funny feeling ran through me. Brie—a name I'd not heard or thought of for a long time. I thought back to the night of that party. That was the night that began a summer I'd not forgotten. "Yeah, well, Brie isn't me, now is she," I said, looking at my sister.

"No, but..." Diane looked away, and I knew she wanted to change the subject.

I cleared my throat. "Brie, how is she? You still talk to her?"

"She's my best friend. Of course I still talk to her."

I nodded, softly smiling at the memory of her. "Is she still in Eastport?"

Diane nodded. "Yes."

"What's she up to now?"

"What's with all the questions?"

"Look, you don't want to talk about Leo. Can I not be curious about people?"

Diane let out a breath. "If you must know, she runs a very successful business here in town, and she has a little one."

I nodded, disappointment filling me. The first girl, maybe the only girl, I'd fallen in love with was now someone else's woman, and I had no one to blame but myself. I could have had her. I had every opportunity to have her, and I'd blown it by leaving her here.

"That's good. Guess I'll have to give those guys a call, maybe get the old crew together for a poker night or something," I said, changing the subject immediately.

"Just don't invite Leo, okay." Diane laughed.

"Don't think you need to worry about that," I bit out. We both grew silent as we sat at the table, my mind going back to Brielle.

"Good to have you home," Diane said, getting up and coming around the table to give me a hug.

"Good to be home," I said, hugging her back.

"You guys ready to eat?" Mom asked, coming into the kitchen and making her way to where the roast was resting on the counter.

"Absolutely," we both said in unison and made our way to the dining room table.

I KISSED HER LIPS, GENTLY FORCING THEM OPEN WITH MY tongue. Her body was pressed against mine, and her hands rested on my ass, pulling me closer.

Our lips parted, and I opened my eyes and brought my hand to her face, brushing her hair back. I looked into her blue eyes, hoping to see something in them other than of want and need, but there was nothing.

I met her lips again, this time taking my time with that kiss. Perhaps she would pick up on how I was beginning to feel about her. As our lips danced over one another, I pulled her close to me, and then gently rolled her onto her back. I reached for the condom that lay on my nightstand, pulling away from her long enough to slip it on.

I took my time with her. This wasn't just about sex anymore for me. I wanted her, every single inch of her, in every way possible. I slid myself into her, and the moan she released went straight through me. I loved it when she made that sound.

I pumped slow and deep, grabbing her ass with one hand, as I held her with the other and kissed her lips. We stayed that way, her legs wrapped around my waist, until we both came.

I walked her to the front door, the sun shining through the windows. I leaned against the wall and watched her as she slid her shoes on and then grabbed her jacket before turning to me. She looked so sexy in the sunlight with her disheveled hair and that 'I just got laid' look in her eyes.

"Thank you for dinner, and a fabulous night," she said, taking a step closer to me. I could already smell a mix of her coconut body lotion mixed with her natural scent.

"My pleasure."

She leaned in and kissed me.

"What are you doing later tonight?" I asked.

"Diane wants to hit the club tonight."

Alarm filled me at the thought of her going to a club. I needed to tell her how I felt, no matter if she didn't return the feelings. I looked down to the floor and then back up to her eyes.

"Oh, I was going to see if you wanted to maybe watch a movie or something."

I watched as a soft smile came to her lips. "What am I going to tell your sister?" She giggled.

"Tell her you have the flu." I shrugged.

"But I already told her I'd go."

"You know you shouldn't lie to your best friend." I chuckled, leaning in and kissing her lips.

She leaned in and kissed me and then pulled away, her eyes still closed.

"Brie, I…"

I woke with a start and looked around the dark room. I ran my hand across my face. I was covered in a sheen of sweat. I blew out a deep breath and kicked the covers off me, getting up to get a drink of water. I looked at myself in the mirror and shook my head. I'd been back in Eastport one week, and I was already thinking of her and all I'd allowed to slip from my fingers.

4

BRIELLE

DREW PLACED his hand on my back and guided me into the restaurant. Once we were seated, I pulled my phone from my purse and checked my messages. I had nothing from the sitter, only one from Diane telling me to relax and enjoy myself. I rolled my eyes, shoved my phone back in my purse, and picked up the menu.

"Everything okay?" Drew asked, looking over the edge of the menu at me.

I nodded. "Yes, of course. Why?"

"Well, for starters, you've checked your phone more in the last half hour than you have spoken to me."

"I'm sorry. Emma is with a new sitter. It's just making me a little uncomfortable." I'd almost canceled when I was unable to book my mom. Diane was working, and my normal sitter couldn't watch Emma either.

Instead, Brenda, one of my employees, had heard I was in a bind and offered to sit with her for the night.

At first, I had said no, but with Diane sitting across from me in the kitchen of The Cooling Rack giving me the look of death when Brenda offered, I decided against it. Now I sat across from a very attractive young doctor perusing a menu, while my knee was continuously hitting the table from nerves.

"Brielle?" he questioned, not looking up from the menu.

"Hmmm..." I mumbled, pretending that I didn't notice that the table was shaking.

"You're nervous. Your knee has hit that table more times than I can count."

"I'm sorry. I'm not used to leaving Emma late at night."

"I'm sure she is in very capable hands."

"She is. I'm sorry. I will try and get a hold of myself. Sorry."

"It's okay. No need to be sorry. I understand. Just try to relax and have a good time. Now, what are you eying on the menu?"

"The chicken looks good. What about you?" I said as I felt my phone vibrate in my purse.

"I think I'm going to have the steak."

"That sounds good too," I answered as, once again, my phone vibrated.

We were halfway through dinner and were in deep conversation when I felt my phone vibrate against my leg for the third time. I did my best to quell the anxiety I could feel building inside of me and continued listening to what he was saying. It worked until I felt the phone begin to continuously vibrate. I knew he could tell something was wrong because he sat there looking at me with concern in his eyes.

"Brielle, just answer your phone," he bit out, raising his glass and taking a sip of wine.

It was that moment I felt the phone vibrate again. "I'm sorry. I'm worried that something is wrong with Emma. Just give me two seconds."

Drew nodded, placing his napkin on the table, and glanced around the restaurant. He was annoyed, and really, I couldn't blame him. This was extremely unfair to him, but I didn't care. I ignored the looks he was giving me and dove into my purse. I unlocked the phone and read the text that sat on my screen, my heart in my throat.

"Oh my God, Emma is on her way to the emergency room. She fell off the jungle gym at the park," I said, panicked as I dialed Brenda's number.

"Just relax and breathe, find out what is going on," Drew said, trying to keep me calm. "I can always call ahead and notify the doctor to update you," he offered.

I could barely contain myself and gathered my

purse. "Sorry, I'm going to have to go," I mumbled, trying hard not to panic as I waited for her to answer her phone.

"I don't think we need to go," he said, annoyed.

"You're wrong. We do," I said.

I looked at Drew just as he rolled his eyes and let out an annoyed huff and signaled the waiter for the check. This was the exact reason why I didn't date. Aside from having no time to build a relationship, I didn't need some guy trying to tell me to calm down. Emma was and would always be my number-one priority, and as a pediatrician, he should have understood that. Instead, I felt as if I were sitting here with a guy who'd never met a parent before. I never left her with strangers, and this was why.

Drew drove straight to Eastport General and followed me in against my wishes. He led the way to the emergency room and over to the nurse's station, and immediately, they directed me to the room where Brenda sat with Emma.

"I'll go try and find out who's looking after her," Drew said, heading off in another direction.

The moment Emma saw me, she held her little arms out and tears began pouring down her cheeks. "Emma, sweetheart, what happened?" I said, sitting down beside Brenda, taking Emma from her and pulling her into my lap, trying to console her.

"She fell off the jungle gym and started crying. Her arm started to swell, and no matter what I did, I couldn't get her to stop crying. I panicked. I didn't know what else to do."

"It's okay, hon, you did exactly what you were supposed to do. Here..." I said, digging in my purse for my wallet, "You don't need to stay. I can take it from here." I handed her the money I owed her for the night.

"No, Brielle, I won't take it. I ruined your date, and on top of that, I broke your child," she said, refusing to take the money from me.

"Brenda, it's okay. It was sort of boring, and Emma will be fine." I winked at her, encouraging her to take the money. A slight smile landed on her lips as Emma began to fuss.

"Seriously, Emma is going to be fine. These kids are made of rubber," I said, pulling her closer to me as Brenda finally took the money I'd offered.

"Thanks, Brielle."

The curtain opened, and Drew smiled down at Emma and me. "So it looks like you'll be in good hands. You'll be looked after by the new transfer. He should be in shortly. I've worked with him a couple of times. He is excellent. Very, very good with kids."

"Thanks, Drew," I said, looking up at him, suddenly feeling bad for how the night had ended.

"Should I call you to reschedule?"

I didn't have the heart to tell the man no, so I just nodded and smiled at him. I knew I'd never hear from him again, I could tell, so I didn't really worry about. "I look forward to it."

Drew gave me half a smile and then looked to Brenda. "Did you need help finding your way out of the hospital?"

Brenda nodded, quickly hugged me, and then followed Drew. I pulled Emma against me, as she rested her head on my shoulder. I smoothed her hair and closed my eyes, waiting for the doctor. I'd finally gotten her calmed down when the curtain parted and Diane rushed into the room, panicked and muttering to herself under her breath.

"Brielle, oh my goodness, I saw Emma's name and rushed in as soon as I could. I must have been with a patient when she came in or I'd of been here right away. I didn't expect to see you here though. They said she was brought in by Brenda."

I let out a laugh. "Brenda called me. She didn't know what else to do."

"What about your date?" she whispered as she took Emma from me and placed her on the exam table, looking her over just like she did every time she got hurt.

"Let's not talk about it okay. He was more annoyed

at the fact that the date was interrupted. I can't date someone who can't understand and accept that she is my main priority," I said as Diane continued examining her.

"I understand. All right, I have to get back to work. I don't know who you are seeing, but the doctor should be in shortly. Here, if she is cold you can use this blanket," Diane said, pulling a blanket from under the exam table.

I grabbed Emma off the table and sat back down in the chair, wrapping the blanket around her. She shoved her thumb in her mouth and buried her face in my neck. Diane smiled at me, tousled Emma's dark hair, kissed her on the cheek, and then left the room.

5

SAWYER

I'D BEEN BACK in Eastport three weeks, and this had been the first ten-day stretch I'd done. I was exhausted and looking forward to my days off. Every night for a week I'd dreamt of Brielle, but they had finally stopped. I walked in behind the nurses' station and handed the current patient file over to one of the nurses.

"Please order these tests and put a rush on them."

"Sure thing."

I'd just sat down and taken my first sip of hot coffee when I heard my name.

"Dr. McKay, your next patient is over in room three." Mandy, the nurse I had been partnered with tonight, handed over a file to me.

"Mandy, please, it's Sawyer. Now, what's it look like?"

"Possible strain or break. Little girl fell off a jungle gym at a park."

"Age?"

"Four."

"Did you order x-rays? You can't be too careful with a child that age."

"I wasn't sure it would be necessary, but I can if you'd like."

"It's okay. Just wait until I take a look. Can you please set up an IV on the patient in room five and start the paperwork to admit Mrs. Rodriguez in room seven. I'm also waiting on a list of tests for room one. Please let me know as soon as those come in."

"Of course. I was just going to take you to room three."

"No need, Mandy, it's fine."

"Well, it's just she is Diane's best friend. She asked me to update her."

"Diane, as in my sister?"

Mandy nodded. "Yes, she just stopped by before you got here."

"My sister is best friends with a four-year-old?"

"No, she is best friends with the mother."

"It's fine. You go, take care of that, and come back

when you're finished. I will update my sister," I said, turning and making my way toward room three.

I stopped outside of the room and washed my hands, then opened the file, quickly reading it over, paying no attention to names and ages. I parted the curtain and stepped into the room, and immediately sat down at the computer without making eye contact.

"I'm Dr. McKay. I will be looking after Emma tonight. So, looks like we have a right-arm injury, or more specific, wrist. Fell off a jungle gym, is that correct?" I said as I logged into the computer and pulled up the patient's electronic chart.

When I didn't get an immediate answer, I put my pen down and turned to look at the patient. The little girl with hair as dark as mine sat huddled against her mother's chest. I raised my eyes to her face, and when they met hers, I froze. Brielle sat across from me. It was almost as if I had been transported back through time, and every feeling I'd ever had for her hit me straight in the gut. She was more beautiful than I remembered.

"Sawyer?" she questioned, her eyes wide, her flushed cheeks turning pale. "What are you doing here?"

"Brielle?" I looked at her, and then glanced down to the little girl on her lap. In a matter of seconds, I was transported to the last few times we had been together. Then I looked back at the computer screen, my eyes skimming over all the information in front of me, looking specifically for the birthdate. I finally found it: June 19, 2018. I quickly did a little math and then the realization hit. It had been a little over four years since I had last laid eyes on her.

I checked Emma's birthdate again and swallowed hard. Was I staring at my child? The condom had broken twice…or had it been three times? I couldn't remember. Could it be possible? Did I have a child I knew nothing about? Had she kept this a secret from me? Suddenly, anger came over me that I could barely control. I slammed the folder shut, got up, and walked out of the room without a word.

I walked down the hall with purpose to the nurses' desk and looked at the girl behind the counter. "Where is Dr. Richards?" I demanded.

"He's in the middle of an emergency that just came in. He says he will be a while and asks that you take over the couple of patients he has so that he can leave once he is finished. Is something wrong?"

"What about Reggie?"

"He, too, is wrapped up with a patient."

As quickly as the idea had flown into my head to have one of them look after Emma, it had been cut out from under me. I was the only doctor available tonight, and I had no choice but to deal with the situation.

"No, everything is fine. I just had a question, but I can figure it out. Thanks."

I needed to get myself and my emotions under control, I thought. I turned and began making my way back down to room three. I blew out a breath. I had no proof that that gorgeous little girl in that room was indeed mine. For all I knew, Brielle had met someone shortly after I'd left and was now happily married, just like Diane had said.

I stood outside of the room and let out a breath before walking back in. I needed to push all that nonsense to the back of my mind so that I could do my job. After all, she had been the one not to call me back.

I blew out a breath and went to the sink and washed my hands again and was just about to head back in when Diane came around the corner.

"Is everything okay, Sawyer?" my sister asked quietly.

I stepped into the supply room without saying anything, pretending to look for a couple of forms, pretending I didn't hear a word my sister had said.

"Sawyer, didn't you hear me?"

"I heard you, Diane. I'm fine."

"You seem bothered with something."

"I guess you could say I am bothered with the way fate has come back to haunt me. Perhaps coming back to Eastport was a mistake." I pulled the forms I had been looking for.

"What the hell is that supposed to mean?" she questioned, a confused look on her face.

"Brielle, is she by any chance married?"

"Brielle? Gosh no. I've tried to fix her up, but I've been unsuccessful. It's too bad. She is such a nice girl."

I nodded, still searching for a form. "Do you happen to know who her child's father is?"

Diane was quiet for a moment. "Sawyer, what is wrong with you? Those are some pretty personal questions." Diane frowned, looking at me as if I'd lost my mind.

"I realize that. It's just her file has no father's name on there. I think the father should know about the incident, don't you?" I said, looking at her for any sign she may give me that the child was mine.

"Why would that be?" she said, crossing her arms in front of her.

I looked to my sister and then to the floor. How was I going to get myself out of this? I shifted my weight from my left to right foot.

"Sawyer, you and I have both known Brielle since school. If you think she did something to that little button, you are crazy."

"That isn't why I am asking," I bit out.

"Well, that should be the only reason you are

asking, and since there is no sign of that, you haven't any right to ask. Look. I have no right to say anything, but I was with Brielle when Emma was born. I can assure you that the father is not now, nor was he ever in the picture. He was a drunken mistake, a one-night stand, completely gone the next day. She hasn't had it easy, and for you to think such a thing would crush her. Besides, Brielle has emergency contacts listed, her mother, and myself," Diane said, shaking her head and turning away from me. "Oh, and any other information you feel you need ,I think you should speak directly with Brielle. Now, I need to go and check on some tests that Dr. Richards ordered."

I leaned against the doorframe and watched my sister walk down the hall. Diane was right; I had no right to ask her any of those questions. I blew out a breath, gathered myself, and walked into room three. Emma was lying on the exam table, covered with a blanket, while Brielle sat beside her holding her little hand and singing a nursery rhyme. She immediately stopped and looked at me.

"Sorry, I had to take care of something. I'd like to examine her wrist if I may," I said, meeting Brielle's eyes.

"Of course." She moved over so I could get in beside Emma.

I looked down at Emma, her bright-blue eyes

staring back at me. I gently took her little hand in mine and moved her wrist, but the slightest movement resulted in Emma screaming out in pain.

"I will put in a call to radiology to get some x-rays," I said, frowning as Emma let out another loud scream.

"You don't think it's broken, do you?" Brielle asked, worry lining her voice.

"Better to be safe than sorry. Judging from the way she just screamed, I'm thinking it might be," I murmured and quickly began filling out a form while Brielle comforted Emma.

It seemed to take forever as I filled out papers I'd filled out millions of times over the past five years. I could feel myself getting hot as I scribbled my signature on the bottom of the form. The tension in the room could have been cut with a knife. I really just wanted to get out of here, and then I heard her clear her throat.

"When did you get back in town?" Brielle asked, finally looking my way.

"A month ago or so. I didn't figure you'd still be living here. I imagined you were off somewhere in some big court room fighting cases left and right." I scribbled out a couple of notes and then closed the file, finally meeting her eyes, only to see sadness in them I'd not seen before.

"Yeah, well, let's just say things didn't turn out the

way I thought they would." She set Emma back down on the table, covering her with the blanket.

I looked to Brielle and nodded. "Radiology should be down in a few minutes. You can go up with her if you'd like, or grab a coffee in the cafeteria. Totally up to you. They will bring her back here, and then I'll be back after the x-ray results are here."

"Thanks, Sawyer."

"You are welcome," I replied and picked up the file. I was about to leave the room, but instead I just stood in the doorway for a moment, before turning back around to look down at them. Brielle sat holding Emma, rocking her gently back and forth, humming away to her.

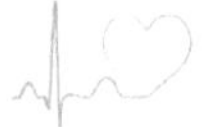

AN HOUR LATER, BRIELLE WALKED BESIDE ME CARRYING a sleeping Emma in her arms. "So, as I said, nothing was broken. It's just a bad sprain."

Brielle nodded. "What about pain?"

"You can give her some children's pain medication every six hours or so. Otherwise, I think she will be okay," I said, looking into her eyes; they were lined with worry. "She may get a fever, so, if you're worried about anything, you can always call me," I said, holding out my card for her to take.

"Thanks, Sawyer. You've been great," she said, taking my card and looking down at it.

"My pleasure." I took hold of her hand and looked into her eyes as a moment of silence passed between us. "Listen, there are some things we should probably talk about."

She pulled her hand away and looked to the floor. "What did you have in mind?"

I had done my best to put the thought out of my mind that Emma was possibly mine, but somehow, deep down, I knew I needed to know for sure. "Tell me when you are available, and we can meet somewhere?"

"Hmmm okay, well, how about Wednesday after-noon? Could you meet me at Eastport Park around two?"

I nodded, "Sure. I will see you then."

"Okay, I'm going to get her home and into bed. Good night."

"Good night, Brielle."

I watched as she turned away from me and carried a sleeping Emma down the hall and away from me. Once she was out of my sight, I heard my name being paged. I stood there for a moment, thinking of what the probabilities were that Emma was indeed mine, and then shook the thought from my head once again.

There was no way she would have kept something like that from me.

Diane was probably right; a one-night stand shortly after I'd left was more than likely the truth. She probably was open to meeting me because she wanted closure, I thought to myself, closure I had never been able to provide, even for myself. I had two days to figure out how I was going to give that to her. My mind was riddled with thoughts when I heard my name again over the paging system.

"Doctor McKay, please report to Emergency."

6

BRIELLE

I'D WORKED on autopilot over the next few days. Emma had been cranky and clingy and only wanted to be with me. I'd been super busy at The Cooling Rack with large orders, but none of that compared to the stress I'd felt after seeing Sawyer. Not only had the journal brought back memories, but now that I'd seen him, I'd dreamt about him every single night since.

I arrived at the park early and set us up along the edge of the beach. I threw down the beach blanket and umbrella and then sat Emma down and dumped out her beach toys in front of her before setting up my chair.

"Emma, did you want a drink?" I asked, watching as she dug her little shovel into the sand.

She looked up at me and nodded her head and

raised her little sand-covered hand to me. I quickly pulled out her cup and handed it to her and watched as she took a drink and then handed me the cup back. I then pulled my book from my bag, turned to where I had left off, and sat back, trying to take my mind off everything.

Emma was finally playing and I had just gotten into the chapter, when I caught movement out of the corner of my eye. I glanced in the direction of the parking lot and saw Sawyer walking across the park in our direction carrying a chair. I couldn't help but take him in. He looked different than he had the other night. Of course, in my panic, I hadn't really taken a close look. He was built a little heavier than when we had been together, like he had been working out. He wore dark-blue jeans and a light long-sleeved shirt that hugged him in all the right places. However, no matter how good he looked, I'd be lying if I said I had been looking forward to this meeting. How I went from being absolutely sure I would never see him again to meeting up with him alone I didn't know. I swallowed hard and put my face back in my book. The last thing I wanted was for him to see me watching him.

It only took him mere minutes to cross the park, and now he stood beside me. He set up his chair and placed it close to mine, then sat down. He said nothing at first. Instead he just sat there studying Emma, probably to see if he could see himself in her actions. Sawyer wasn't a stupid man, and I was surprised that he didn't ask me the other night in the emergency room. He was going to be in for a big surprise because as she sat there struggling with her little shovel, every expression that lined her face was his.

"How is she today?" he questioned, still watching her.

"She had a bit of a fever through the night, but it eventually broke this morning. I've followed your suggestion with the medication, and she says her arm doesn't hurt anymore."

"I'm glad to hear that."

He was silent again, still studying her, a small smile on his lips as he watched her dump over her bucket and begin filling it again. He could tell, I knew he could, and I swallowed hard, trying to come up with a way to tell him.

"Why didn't you tell me about her?"

So this was how we were going to do this. Neither of us able to swim, we were going to jump right on into the deep end of the pool without a life jacket. I let out a deep breath and placed my book down on top of my bag. "I guess you could say I didn't want to interfere with your dream or your goals."

"Are you serious?" He glared at me with disbelief. "Like really serious?"

I nodded. "Yes, Sawyer. I couldn't do that to you. You had worked so hard."

Sawyer chuckled to himself and ran his hand across the back of his neck. "So in your mind it's okay that you kept something like this from me? It's okay that our daughter would grow up never knowing her father?"

I didn't say anything. I could see the anger in his face.

"We aren't talking about a puppy, Brielle. We are talking about a child."

"I am fully aware of what we are talking about."

"Are you? I'm not sure you do. Do you have any idea how I feel about this? Let me tell you, I feel like shit because I wasn't there for you when you needed me. I also haven't been there for her. I've missed out on raising my daughter, missing birthdays and holidays, because you chose not to tell me."

"There is no reason for you to feel like shit, Sawyer. I made the choice—for both of us. Being a doctor was your dream, and you have the right to live it."

"Well, you had no right to make that choice for me. None. We could have made it work, and besides, you had dreams too, Brielle. What makes it right for you to give up yours?"

I thought for a moment. "I didn't give them up. I

just slightly altered them. I didn't really have a choice, but you did."

"Oh come on, like I said, you made the choice for you, but you had no right to make it for me." Tension lined his shoulders as he looked off into the distance.

"Sawyer, we spent one summer together screwing around. It wasn't like we were in a serious, committed relationship. There wasn't a soul who knew about us. Hell, to this day, Diane still doesn't know. You were leaving, and to be honest, I was very unsure of what we even were to one another, if anything at all."

"So my hints weren't strong enough?"

"What hints?"

"Movies, dinners alone, making excuses not to go out with friends or to leave a party early. That I still wanted to see you?"

I couldn't help but chuckle. "You wanted someone to keep your bed warm, and sure you wanted to see me when you came home on break."

"Brielle, don't you dare try and downplay this. I never ever treated you like you were an object, *ever*. You also know that I didn't mean it like that either."

"How did you mean it then?"

Sawyer ran his hand over his face, and I could see the tension in his jaw. "Jesus, Brielle, if you must know, I was in love with you. I didn't know how else to broach the subject. I had planned on returning from that internship, figuring by then we would be serious, and then we could get married and start a family. Instead, I never heard from you again."

"Is that right?"

"Yes."

"Well, Sawyer, perhaps you should have been a little more clear on what you meant," I bit back.

"Tell me one thing: why is that I never heard from you again?"

I looked down at the book that sat in my lap.

"Tell me the truth, was there someone else?"

"No, Sawyer, there was no one else." I was hurt that he would even think that way of me.

"Then what was it?"

"Sawyer, after I dropped out of school, I flew out to Seattle. It was about a month after you had left. I wanted to surprise you, and that was when I planned on telling you about the baby. I had it all played out in my mind, that you would be happy and ask me to move in with you. Instead, when I arrived, I saw you with a nurse. You were walking back to your apartment, she hung off your arm, you were both laughing and talking. I didn't have the strength to even get out of the car after seeing her all over you. Instead I had the driver take me back to the airport. My heart was crushed. It wasn't as if I didn't expect that you would date, but seeing you with her, well, I couldn't face it. So you can tell me whatever you want. You can say you loved me, but I have a hard time believing that."

"So you think because you saw me with some girl that my feelings for you weren't true."

"Sure looked like it."

"Well, Brielle, you are wrong. She was the sister of the doctor I was rooming with. She asked if she could walk with me so she could see her brother, and on the way, she twisted her ankle. That was why she was holding onto my arm and she was walking with me because the neighborhood that we lived in wasn't exactly the safest place on the earth."

I felt my stomach drop at his admission.

"And, just so you know, I tried to call you, Brielle, a lot. You never took my calls, nor did you once ever call back. I came home many times in the five years I was gone, and every single time I thought about coming to see you but knew damn well I'd be wasting my time because you wouldn't see me."

He was right, I wouldn't have seen him, because then he would have known about the baby.

"You weren't fair to me, Brielle. But regardless of what happened between us, together or not, I still had every right to know about her," he said, glancing to Emma. "Every right."

I didn't know what to say. I had planned on him

never finding out because I had planned on never seeing him again.

I looked down to where my hands were clasped in my lap. "I know," I whispered.

"I feel like I need to do something, to help you out in some way."

"The last thing I need or want is charity, Sawyer. I've done fine supporting both of us all this time. We are fine."

Sawyer looked at me, a frown coming to his face. "Brielle, she is my daughter. I have a right to be involved somehow."

I looked down to Emma and then leaned forward toward Sawyer. "You were involved for about fifteen minutes."

"That isn't what I meant, Brielle, and you know it. Stop acting as if I am the enemy here. I am trying to tell you I want to be a part of this," Sawyer bit out, looking me directly in the eyes.

I turned and looked out at the water, doing my best to calm myself down. There was nothing to fix. He had no right to start demanding to be a part of her life, but on the other hand, I had no right to deny him either. I also had no right to treat him the way I was.

"I can only imagine what your mother must think of me," Sawyer mumbled.

I turned and looked at him. I could see the hurt splashed across his face. "My mom doesn't know."

"How does your mother not know? Let me guess, you were like those women on that show *I Didn't Know I was Pregnant*."

"I mean she doesn't know that Emma is yours. As I said, Diane doesn't even know. I kept our secret, just like you wanted. All my mother knows was that we hung out sometimes with our friends. She did ask me if you were the father because she thought something was going on between us, but I flat out denied it. I told my mother that Emma was the result of a drunken one-night stand and that the father wanted nothing to do with me or the baby afterward."

"Lord, Brielle, I'm sure your mother could do math."

I shook my head. "Once Emma was born, she questioned it again, but I made up a date and told her the one-night stand happened right before you left."

"Are you ever going to tell her?"

"I wasn't planning on it, no. Besides, you were never supposed to come back to Eastport."

"Well, I'm here now," Sawyer said, "and I know about her, and I want to help. I want to be a part of her life. I deserve to be a part of her life."

I closed my eyes for a moment and dug deep inside to pull myself out of this pit I felt I was in. I knew I had been wrong by not telling him, and I realized now how much of a mess I'd really dug myself into. It hadn't just been Sawyer I had lied to, but my mother and my best friend as well.

"Are you planning on staying in Eastport?" I asked, looking to Sawyer.

When he didn't answer me right away, I knew the answer. He had probably taken the position at Eastport General as a stepping stone to get into another position in another hospital somewhere in the world. If that was the case, I wouldn't let him near Emma.

"What is that supposed to mean?"

"Look, I don't want you to be in and out of her life. I know firsthand what it's like to have a father walk out, so I refuse to do that to her."

"So you're going to paint me with the same brush I see."

"No, I never said that, but if you are going to be her dad then you need to understand it's a full-time job. You are either here or you're not. Once a routine is established, she won't understand why you don't show up when it's your turn to have her, and she certainly won't understand why all of a sudden you aren't around anymore either."

"If you are asking me if I'm back in Eastport for good, Brielle, the answer is yes. I missed home too much to leave again."

I looked into his dark-brown eyes, trying to read them. It had been so long since I had seen him, and I was feeling so out of touch with myself after all that had happened over the past few days that I couldn't quite tell if he was just saying that or if he meant it.

"I don't know, Sawyer," I murmured.

"Mommy, look!" Emma shouted.

When I didn't immediately look, she stood up and came over to me, pulling my shirt. I tore my eyes from Sawyer and pulled her against me, kissing her forehead. "Yes, I see it, baby. It's a bird."

She pulled her little hands into her chest and laughed as the bird ran down the beach.

"Why don't you get back down and play in the sand," I whispered, kissing her forehead.

She looked at Sawyer with curiosity. "Mommy, who that?" She pointed to Sawyer.

Sawyer smiled at her. "That's just an old friend of Mommy's," I said, pulling her hair from her face. "Now how about you go back and play."

She slid off my lap and went back to digging in the sand and playing with her toys. I smiled at her, until I realized that by forcing her back down, I was back to the reality and that the conversation Sawyer and I were having was still staring me in the face. I turned to face him only to see the pain in his eyes.

"Brielle, please, let me try. Let me try and prove to you how serious I am about this."

"How would you like to do that?"

"How about a date? Just you and me where we can talk."

I couldn't help but laugh to myself, at how naive Sawyer truly was when it came to what it was like to have a child. "Well, Sawyer, as wonderful as that sounds, I just can't leave a four-year-old unattended, and I don't have a sitter."

"All right, well, then why don't we take Emma to the fall fair? You and me."

I had planned on taking her myself the following weekend. I shrugged. "I guess we could do that."

"Okay, so I will pick you both up early next Saturday morning."

I quickly ran through my schedule and shook my head. "It will have to be after eleven." I had orders to prepare at work. Plus, I had to open the bakery.

"Okay, how about two o'clock?"

"Fine, Sawyer, two o'clock," I said, meeting his eyes.

"Now will you do me a favor and introduce me to my daughter," he pleaded.

Sawyer had called every day since we had met a week ago to check on Emma. It was Wednesday morning and I was expecting him to call and cancel our day trip on Saturday. Yet he shocked me when he'd come by on Wednesday night and brought dinner with him after Emma was already tucked into bed.

That time together had given us a chance to clear the air between us. We spent the evening getting reacquainted, not arguing. After he had left, I sat in the darkness of my living room wishing that somehow things had turned out differently. I was tired of struggling. I was tired of upholding a lie to the people who mattered. Perhaps this was the chance.

A little after two on Saturday, I saw his car pull up out front of my apartment building. I carried Emma out to his car and was just about to tell him I would drive, so I didn't need to grab the car seat, but when I poked my head in the window, I was surprised to find there was a car seat already in the back.

"I picked it up from the store yesterday," he said, climbing out of the driver's seat and coming around to grab my bag and stroller.

"Wow, Sawyer, you didn't have to do that."

"I did. I told you I wanted to be a part of this and I meant it." His eyes meant mine.

I watched him for a minute as he loaded everything

into the trunk and then came over to my side. "Here, give her to me."

"I can put her in the car seat," I said, but I could tell he wasn't going to back down, so I handed Emma over and watched as he strapped her in and then placed her blanket over her legs.

"All set," he said, stepping around me and pulling my door open, waiting until I climbed into the front seat. I watched as Sawyer ran around the front of the car and climbed into the driver's seat.

Once we arrived at the fair, Sawyer insisted on heading over to the rides that were geared for small kids. He purchased tickets and went with her on every ride, holding her on his lap while I watched from a distance. I could tell she liked him; she never made a fuss and was always smiling any time he would show her any attention. Then she wrapped her little arms around his neck and hung onto him as we made our way to the next ride. She would throw her head back and laugh while he held her tight.

Once he'd taken her on every ride, he stopped and grabbed tickets for the games. There was a little magnet fishing game that she was insistent on playing all because she wanted a big Minnie Mouse stuffed toy. When she didn't win, she burst into tears.

Sawyer looked at me and then down to Emma whose chubby little cheeks were streaked with tears.

"Do you really want that Minnie?" Sawyer asked, kneeling down to her eye level.

She nodded.

"Then just you wait." He took off in the direction of the ticket guy before I could stop him.

I remembered he had done this with me one night. Of course I never broke down into tears, but I remembered he had spent over a hundred dollars trying to win my something at this exact fair, when finally the guy behind the counter took pity on him and just gave him what he had wanted because of all the money he had spent.

I picked Emma up and wiped her tears, then grabbed her juice and handed her her bottle. Within minutes, Sawyer was back with another handful of tickets. He looked around and saw a ring toss game that had the exact same Minnie hanging from the rafters. "Let's go over there." He nodded.

"All right." I strapped Emma into her stroller and covered her with a blanket, and then followed Sawyer over to where he stood, with a handful of rings, already beginning to play.

"Hopefully, you've gotten better at this game," I called, smiling at him.

"I'm surprised you remembered. Now let's hope I am." He laughed.

A half hour later, he finally landed the third and

final ring on the bottle needed to win the Minnie Mouse. He turned and smiled at me, then pointed to the stuffed animal. The game attendant reached up and grabbed it and handed it to Sawyer.

I smiled and shook my head. "I can't believe you did that for her."

"She will be so surprised when she wakes up."

"So tell me, how much did that end up costing you?" I questioned.

"Believe me, you don't want to know." Sawyer laughed and glanced down at his watch. "Did you want to go and watch the fireworks before we head back?"

I smiled and nodded. "That sounds wonderful."

Sawyer reached over and placed his hand over mine, and a surge of electricity pulsed through me. I slowly let go of Emma's stroller and let him take it. He lifted his left arm, waiting for me to slide mine through his, just like he always did when we had gone anywhere. I was hesitant at first, and then slipped my arm through his. We walked that way to the end of the beach where we found an empty bench away from the crowd.

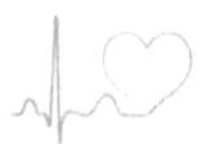

Sawyer pulled into the parking lot of my apartment building and pulled into one of the visitors spots and cut the engine.

"Thank you so much for today. I had an amazing time."

"No, Brie, thank you," he said, his voice quiet and deep as he stared at me.

A funny feeling went through me as he used the short form of my name. He was the only one I'd ever allowed to call me that. I met his eyes and then glanced in the back seat at a sleeping Emma. "If you give me a couple of minutes, I will just take in all the stuff and then come down to get her."

"I can bring her up if you like," he whispered.

"It's late, Sawyer, and you have to work in the morning."

He shrugged. "It's okay. I've spent many days being tired at work because of worse choices. I'll be fine. I don't mind."

I smiled and nodded. No doubt he was telling me the truth. I was tired anyway and could use the help. We climbed out of the car together, he pulled the stroller, bag, and stuffed animal out of the trunk, then walked around to the passenger's side of the car and reached in. He gently picked her up, careful not to wake her, and rested her against his chest.

My stomach flopped at the sight of him holding

our baby, her little fist up to her mouth as she sucked on her thumb. He carried her up to my apartment, and I was shocked that she still hadn't woken. I opened the door and walked in, flipping the light on in the corner of the living room.

"Where is her room?" Sawyer whispered, looking around my small but cozy apartment.

"Right over there," I whispered, pointing to the far door.

He slipped his shoes off and carried her over to her bedroom door. He was just about to step inside when she started to whine.

"Did you want me to take her?" I questioned, beginning to make my way over to them, but Sawyer shook his head and gently bounced her. She immediately stopped fussing.

"I'm fine. Why don't you make us a cup of coffee or something while I put her down."

I watched as she ground her small fists into her eyes, but Sawyer didn't stop. I stood and listened for a moment. He didn't need to get her in her pajamas because I had done that before we had left the park. Instead, I heard him start to read the same book I had read to her the night before. His deep voice took on this soft tone, and as I stood there listening, I knew that I really had made a mistake keeping her from him.

Tears came to my eyes as I listened for a few more minutes before finally tearing myself away.

I carried two steaming mugs into the living room and placed them on the coffee table. I could still see the soft glow of the light on in Emma's room but could no longer hear Sawyer reading to her. I took a sip of my coffee and was about to get up and go make sure everything was okay when he stepped out of her room, pulling the door closed partway behind him.

He smiled as he made his way over to me and sat down. He picked up his cup and took a sip, then sat back against the couch, not saying a word.

"Everything okay?" I questioned.

"Of course," he said, smiling at me. "She's amazing."

I smiled. "So why did you come back to Eastport?" I questioned as we both took a sip of coffee.

"Honestly, as good as I've made my life in Seattle sound, it was lonely. Plus, Mom and Dad are getting up there. Dad just had knee replacement surgery and had a few complications, and Mom needed help looking after him. I can't do it from there, and Diane has her own problems with that dick she married, which I am sure you know all about, so when the opportunity came up to apply, I did."

"Is your father okay now?" I questioned. I hadn't seen him in a while. His mother sometimes stopped into The Cooling Rack on occasion, but I was always in the back when she came in.

"He's doing better, thanks."

"That's good," I said, picking up my mug. "What about your significant other?" As the words slipped out of my mouth, I wished I could swallow them back down. I didn't want him to think I was interested in anything with him. I more wanted to know what she thought of all this.

"There isn't anyone at the moment. I dated some of the nurses at the hospital in Seattle, but my work schedule was heavy and didn't really permit me to have a private life."

I nodded in understanding.

"What about you? How have things been for you?"

I picked up my mug of coffee and leaned back, pulling the pillow that had sat behind me in front of me as if it were going to form some sort of protective shield around me.

"Things are good now. I won't lie that it's been rough. I had no idea what I was doing when I dropped out of school shortly after I found out I was pregnant. There was no way I would have been able to keep up with the demand of law school, I'd already known that. It took me months to figure out what I was going to do. I knew my mother was angry and there was no way she was going to let me move through life without education.

"After Emma was born, I enrolled into the community college here. I took night courses in business management. When I finally graduated, I worked for a couple bakeries in town but had a hard time keeping the jobs. Mom couldn't always be with Emma, Diane was having issues with her ex, and of course the owners didn't want a baby in my office. I couldn't just leave her with anyone. It needed to be someone that I could trust. So, after six months of shitty pay and a lot of work, I decided that if I was going to be able to support us, the only way I could do it and be successful was by being my own boss.

"So, I went back to night school, completed a pastry chef program and an entrepreneur program. Once I was graduated, I took the remaining money I had saved for law school and got a small business loan and put it all towards opening The Cooling Rack."

"Diane said you owned a successful business, but I had no idea that it was The Cooling Rack," he said.

"Yep, that's my baby. I pour all my blood, sweat and tears into that place."

"How did I not know that? I stop by there almost every morning for breakfast, and sometimes for dinner when I tire of cafeteria food. I've never seen you there."

"So do most doctors. I'm surprised you didn't know because Diane tells everyone." I giggled. "I'm normally in the back doing bookwork, baking, and running the kitchen. I leave most of the front of the store to the staff."

Sawyer looked down to where his hands rested in his lap. "Is it going okay? I mean, are you making enough to support yourselves?"

"It's been challenging, and had its moments. I almost lost it twice, but after a few tweaks, yes, I am doing better each year. It's a lot of work, but it makes it easy now that Mom is retired and she can stay with Emma most of the time—her or Diane—and when they can't be with her, she just comes with me."

He glanced around the apartment, growing quiet, and then he turned his eyes to me. He sat there a funny look on his face. I watched as his jaw tensed, and then he cleared his throat. "Are you seeing anyone?" he questioned.

I shook my head. "No, Sawyer, I'm not. Diane keeps trying to fix me up with people, even though I beg her not to bother. Most of the men my age are looking for fun, and that is something that I can't do with the responsibility of a baby and a cafe," I said, quickly bringing my hand to my mouth to cover as I let out a yawn.

"I see, well, you have another sitter if you need," he

said, glancing down at his watch. "I really should get going. It's almost eleven, and you probably have to work in the morning."

I nodded. "Yes, I have to be at the café for five." I smiled and watched as Sawyer stood.

I followed him to the door and watched as he slipped his shoes on. Then he turned to me.

"We need to figure out a plan, some way that I can spend time with Emma."

"Sure, why don't you text me your schedule and we will figure something out?"

He turned and looked my way. When our eyes met, an odd silence fell between us. Sawyer looked at me and slowly brought his hand up and brushed away a loose strand of hair that had fallen into my eyes, his hand resting on my cheek. I could feel my heart pounding in my chest at the feel of his warm skin on mine. "I never wanted to be apart from you," he whispered, and without any warning, he leaned in and met my lips.

All the feelings I had worked so hard to bury came rushing back, and as his lips danced over mine, it was like I was transported back five years. His hands rested on my hips, and he brushed his thumb over the soft, bare skin of my abdomen. I could feel a part of me awaken that had been asleep for so long. I wrapped my arms around his shoulders and felt him press his body

Brie smiled. "If you'd like."

She carried Emma over and passed her to me. As always she reached her little arms out and wrapped them around my neck. "Daddy," she squealed.

I looked at Brie, my heart in my throat. This was the first time Emma had called me Daddy. "My God, did you hear that?" I asked, swallowing hard.

"I did." Brie smiled at me, her eyes full of happiness. "Take your daughter and put her to bed," she whispered, kissing Emma good night on the cheek.

I hugged her tighter to me and carried her in her bedroom. I sat down in the rocking chair, sitting her on my lap, and then grabbed two of the books I had gotten her off her little bookshelf.

"Which one would you like to hear tonight?" I said, holding them out in front of her?

She quickly pointed to the bright-pink book, and so I flipped it open and began reading it to her while gently rocking. At first, she was glued to the book, pointing at the pictures, looking up at me, and then she quieted down, and before I had reached the end, she was sound asleep against me.

I carefully scooped her up and placed her in bed, then I covered her up and placed the Minnie Mouse doll I had won for her beside her.

I looked down at her and watched her sleep for a moment. I didn't want to be apart from her any more than I had to, nor did I want to be away from Brie. I wanted to make them a permanent part of my life. I bent down and placed a kiss on Emma's forehead and then switched the light off. Now I just needed to figure out a way to let Brie know I was serious about them.

I made my way back out to the living room and found Brie on the couch almost asleep. I sat down beside her and brushed the hair from her eyes. She stirred and looked up at me with sleep-filled eyes.

"Hey," I whispered.

"Sorry, I must have fallen asleep," she said, trying to push herself up. "Did you get her down all right?"

"Of course I did. Daddy isn't going to fail her." I smiled as I met her eyes.

She studied me for a moment, and then a soft smile came to her lips. "You look so happy."

"I am happy. She is everything, and I can't believe in the short time I have known her that I already feel that way."

"I know that feeling. It's like your entire world changes."

I nodded and looked at her for a moment, then without warning, the words fell from my lips. "There is only one thing that would make me happier."

"What's that?"

"You."

I wasn't sure how she was going to respond to my

answer, but she surprised me by meeting my lips with hers. As she kissed me, she rose onto her knees and pushed me back against the couch so she could straddle me. I kissed her deeply, allowing my hands to run up her back as I pulled her against me. I could feel my cock starting to harden as she lowered herself onto my lap. She surprised me by pulling her shirt off over her head and reached behind her to undo her bra. My eyes roamed her body as she allowed the fabric of her bra to fall away from her body. Her nipples were already hard, and my mouth watered at the thought of sucking one of those perfect buds into my mouth.

I reached behind my head and pulled my shirt off and leaned back on the couch, my eyes meeting hers before they ran over her body once again. I brought my hands up and cupped her breasts, then leaned forward and took one in my mouth. I gently bit the hardened peak. She let out a tiny gasp and wrapped her hand in my hair.

My cock ached behind the zipper of my jeans. I'd felt like I'd had permanent blue balls for the past couple of months. We'd had yet to go further than a little fooling around. I had made a promise to myself that nothing more would happen between us until I was sure she was ready. As I kissed her, I held her hips tight against me, grinding up into her.

I looked into her eyes and traced my fingers down

her stomach to the button on her jeans. I flicked it open with one hand. She rose up onto her knees, and I roughly pulled her jeans down her legs. She placed her hands on my shoulders and looked down into my eyes. I allowed my fingers to gently dance over the fabric of her panties, her body shuddering as I did so. I placed a kiss on either thigh and gripped her ass in my hands.

My cock throbbed as I held her there, teasing her with my tongue through the fabric of her panties. Her fingers dug into my shoulders. I was about to pull the fabric of her panties to the side when she lowered herself back down onto my lap. She looked at me, her eyes full of want, but without another word, she got up off my lap, allowing her jeans to fall to the floor. I frowned as she walked over to her bedroom door and looked back over at me.

"Where are you going?" I questioned, unsure of what was happening here.

But she didn't answer. She just smiled at me and cocked her head toward the bedroom. "Aren't you coming?"

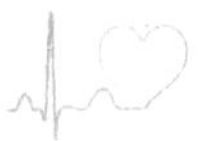

I COULD STILL HEAR THE SOUNDS OF HER ORGASM AS I sat in the quietness of my office. It was a little past eight, and I was working hard to finish up the final bit of paperwork I had before I made my way home for the night, which was proving to be difficult, since I couldn't get her out of my mind. I let out a breath and set the patient file to the side when I heard a knock on my door.

"Come in," I called, not looking up as I heard the door open.

"Sawyer, I am surprised you are still here," Dr. Richards, said looking down to his watch. "I was just going to drop this on your desk, but since you are here, I may as well talk to you about it."

"Sure, come on in. Please have a seat."

Dr. Richards pulled the chair out on the other side of the desk and took a seat, looking a little perplexed at the paperwork in his hand.

"Sawyer, your work in this hospital over the past few months has not gone unnoticed."

"Thank you, sir."

"And I wish there were better opportunities here for someone as hard working as yourself. That being said, at the same time, it would be a shame to lose you. However, there is a position open in a hospital in Florida and they are looking for a supervising doctor to head up their ER."

I sat back in my chair, giving Dr. Richards my full, undivided attention. This position he referred to had been my dream. "When does the application period end?"

"In a couple of weeks, but as your supervisor, I took the liberty of sending in a referral. You are a tremendous doctor, and I would hate to see you lose out on this position."

I looked at Dr. Richards. "I don't really know what to say."

Dr. Richards leaned forward and threw a thick envelope on my desk. Then he sat back and crossed his arms in front of him, smiling.

"What is this?" I asked, looking down to the manila envelope.

"Your offer. The hospital administrator sent this to me this morning. They want you. Take some time and look it all over. You've got lots of time."

I looked down at the envelope that lay on my desk, almost afraid to touch it. Then I looked back up at Dr. Richards just as his name came over the intercom.

"I'll have to think about it, of course," I said.

"Of course. Give it some thought, look over what they sent, and I will see you tomorrow, Sawyer. Congratulations on the offer. It's an amazing opportunity," he said, walking to the door of my office and opening it.

The second he was gone, I looked back down to the thick white envelope that sat on my desk. I picked it up and fiddled with the flap, letting out a deep breath. I knew this envelope held the contents of what I had worked so hard to achieve. I just couldn't bear to open it right now, so I took it and shoved it into my bag and packed up my things.

It was almost nine by the time I got home. I showered and got changed then sat down in the kitchen. I emptied the contents of my bag and sat there with the envelope staring back at me. I blew out a breath and opened it. I sifted through the papers. I was about halfway through the package when my cell phone rang. A smile came to my lips as I saw Brie's name flash across the screen.

"Hello."

"Hey, sorry, I know it's late and you're probably exhausted, but Emma's been crying all evening. She wants to say good night." I could hear the exhaustion in her voice and a crying Emma in the background.

"Put her on." I smiled as I heard Brie say something to Emma.

"Hi, Daddy." She sniffled.

My eyes went right to the package in front of me that held the offer, and I swallowed hard. I shouldn't have bothered even reading it. I should have just flat out denied the offer.

"Hey, angel. You getting ready for bed?"

"Yes, Daddy. When are you coming over?"

"I'll see you tomorrow okay. Now be a good girl for Mommy and crawl into bed."

"I want you to read me a story, Daddy." She sniffled.

This kid was literally breaking my heart. I closed my eyes. "I will read to you tomorrow night. It's Mommy's turn tonight."

"Okay, Daddy."

I could practically see her little face all scrunched up in a pout. I blew out a breath and pinched the bridge of my nose with my fingers as all the stress piled onto me.

"Hey, sorry about that. She's been screaming for you all night. How was your day?"

"Busy as usual. What about yours?"

"Crazy. Will we see you tomorrow?"

I pulled the newspaper overtop of the offer and got up to grab a mug from the cupboard. "You bet you will."

"Okay, we'll see you then. Night, Sawyer."

"Night."

I hung up the phone, made a cup of tea, and stood looking back to where I knew the offer sat. Finally, curiosity got the best of me, and I sat back down to flip through the offer.

8

BRIELLE

Emma sat playing with her toys in my office while I began preparing some orders that were to be picked up for the late morning. The Cooling Rack was buzzing this morning, and I had more orders than normal to pack up. I set up some boxes on the counter and began packing them as I hummed along to the song that played on the radio.

"Someone is rather happy this morning," Brenda said, coming into the kitchen with a bin of dirty mugs and began loading them in the dishwasher.

I giggled. "I guess you could say that."

"All right, spill it. Did you have a date with that guy again? What was his name..." She put her finger up to her lips in thought. "Drew?"

I let out laugh. "No, that ship sailed long ago."

"What has gotten into you then?" Brenda questioned, turning to look at me.

I was about to answer when the back door opened and Sawyer walked in. He was dressed in dark jeans and a white T-shirt that hugged every muscle he had. "Morning," he said, walking over to me and placing a kiss on my lips. "How's it going?"

"Good. Little busier than I expected, but all the baking is finally finished."

Just then Emma let out a loud squeal of excitement. I glanced over and watched as she balanced herself as she got up off the floor, running in Sawyer's direction. He bent down and quickly scooped her up in his arms.

"She probably needs to be changed. She just woke up a little bit ago," I said, wiping my hands on my apron.

"I got her. Where is her diaper bag?"

"Just inside my office door." I nodded.

"All right, let's go, Emma bear," Sawyer said taking her into my office and closing the door behind him.

I looked over at Brenda, who stood there looking at me. "Oh my God, Brielle. I can see why you are so happy... He is hot."

I smiled and nodded.

"Is he..." She nodded to the closed door.

I was about to answer her but stopped speaking

when the door to the kitchen opened and Diane walked in wearing her scrubs.

"Good morning!" she sang as she sat down in her usual spot with a cup of coffee in her hand. She reached across and grabbed a freshly baked cookie off the sheet I was emptying. Diane had been away on a course the past few weeks. In some ways, I'd been thankful because it had given me the chance to spend time with Sawyer without her asking me all kinds of questions.

Brenda took one look at the two of us and excused herself, heading back out to the front.

"What's up?" I questioned once the door had closed behind Brenda.

"I was going to call you, but with the course, I haven't had a chance. I should have told you a long time ago but didn't, and now I pray it isn't too late."

I frowned. "What is it? What's wrong?"

"The night you were in the hospital with Emma, Sawyer was the attending doctor?"

I nodded, focusing on packaging the cookies in front of me.

"Well, he was asking me all kinds of questions about you and Emma. He wanted to know who the father was so he could call him. He said he needed to be notified of the incident."

"It's not what you think," I said, reaching for the next tray of cookies.

"I don't know, Brielle. I thought he was acting weird at first, but I have seen this before with young single parents who come into the hospital with injuries on their children. The attending physicians end up reporting them for abuse. I just want you to be ready in case..."

"Sawyer isn't going to report me, Diane."

"Don't be so sure. I tried to talk him out of it that night. I have been talking with him while I was away. He's been acting funny. He always has to go, and anytime I mention your name, he gets even more weird. I don't trust that he isn't going to. I mean he won't tell me because he'd know I'd kick him right where it counts, not to mention I'd tell you."

A funny feeling hit me in the pit of my stomach. Diane was going to hate me forever, but she needed to know the truth. She sat there shoving another cookie into her mouth with a worried look on her face. "Diane, I have something I want to tell you."

A look of anger came over her face. "Did he already do it? I swear to God I will break every finger on his hands. He'll never operate again." She got up from the seat she was sitting in, pacing back and forth as she ripped another cookie off the sheet in front of me.

I was about to tell her when the door to my office opened and Sawyer walked out carrying a happier Emma in his arms. "She's all changed," he announced, and then looked over to where I stood with Diane.

Diane looked to Sawyer, then to me, then back to Sawyer a confused look on her face. "What is going on here?" Diane asked, her eyes moving back and forth between us.

I looked to Sawyer and held my hand up, letting him know I would handle this. "Diane, I know I told everyone that it was a one-night stand that produced Emma, but it wasn't."

"What! Brielle, what are you talking about?"

"I know who the father is," I said, looking at Diane and then back to Sawyer.

"Who?" she questioned, the color draining from her face as she looked between us, finally figuring it out. "No, don't you dare say it."

"Your brother is Emma's father. It happened the summer before he left for Seattle. We were both single, we were both alone. We were at John Lion's party—you know the one you met Leo at and left early. Well, one thing led to another. Neither of us were ready for a relationship, but we hit it off and one thing led to another, and without warning, we decided to spend the summer messing around. We didn't tell anyone. I found out I was pregnant right before he left for Seattle."

Diane sat there, shock lining her face with the information I'd given. "You're kidding me, right?" she asked, looking at me.

I shook my head. "No, I'm not kidding. Don't be angry with me, please," I begged. "I couldn't handle you being angry with me."

"I'm an aunt?" she asked, shock lining her voice.

"Well, you always have been her Aunt Diane," I answered, looking over at my best friend. I had insisted that Diane be her aunt for a reason.

"No, I mean, like her real aunt?"

I nodded, biting my bottom lip and laughing as I allowed the shock of the information to settle into her mind. I glanced over to Sawyer, who stood there smiling.

"Why didn't neither of you tell me?" Diane asked.

"It's complicated," I answered, pulling another tray of cookies so I could avoid her eyes. "I never told Sawyer about her."

"Wait, you never told him? That's why you were all over me that night with those questions?" she asked, turning to Sawyer.

"Yes. I told you I wasn't going to report her," Sawyer said, coming over to stand beside me. "I took one look at her birth date and put it together. I wanted to know if what I thought was true, but without coming out and asking."

I was silent, and once again I could feel all the guilt climb back into my shoulders.

"Brielle, why wouldn't you have told him?"

"We were young, he was just starting his career, we were only messing around. There are so many reasons. But I am not going to lie, when he came in the room that night at the hospital, I was shocked. I never expected to see him again. He figured it out pretty fast. Your brother never was a stupid guy," I said, leaning into him and placing my hand on his chest. "We met up a few days later and had a talk. We've started seeing one another."

"And?"

I softly smiled while I finished loading the remainder of the cookies into the box and sealing it. "We are working things out."

"That's why you've been acting weird," Diane said, looking to Sawyer.

It had been good for me to have Sawyer back in my life. I was happy to see he really wanted to spend time with his daughter, and in return he was building a relationship with me. At first, I was hesitant. I was so afraid to let him into our little twosome. I didn't want to be hurt again, but I would be able to deal with the heartbreak if he no longer wanted to be a part of us. Emma was a different story. She would never understand if he no longer came around, and until her reaction last night, I didn't realize how quickly she attached herself to him.

"I'm gonna take Emma out to the park and let you two talk. We will be back in an hour," Sawyer said, placing a kiss on my temple.

"Okay, have fun."

I watched as Sawyer made his way out the back door with Emma in his arms. Then I turned back to Diane.

"How is Emma reacting to him?" she questioned.

"Well, last night she wouldn't stop crying until she said good night to him."

Diane let out a laugh. "Sounds like Emma." She grew quiet and then took on a serious look. "What about you?"

"What about me?"

"How are you reacting to him?"

I didn't want to admit what I was feeling to anyone, mainly because there was no way my feelings for him should already or perhaps still be so strong. I'd crushed on Sawyer growing up and I'd never let Diane know. Even after we'd started whatever it was that went on between us, I had done my best to protect my heart. I had been in love with him, and even though I had never wanted to admit that to myself then, I couldn't hide that from myself any longer. Every one of those feelings I'd had before were starting to resurface.

"As I said, we are working on things," I answered before biting into one of the fresh cookies.

I thought about all the time we had been spending together. He was the same guy he'd always been, only now his attention was focused on Emma, which was how it should be because she was the most important person in all of this. I was constantly second-guessing my thoughts on whether or not we would both be able to fit in his life.

"Working on things? Are you two sleeping together?"

I turned around to place the racks into the dishwasher and grabbed the next rack of croissants only so I could hide my face from her. We hadn't slept together yet. We had messed around but that was the extent of it.

"Brielle? Please, I'm not trying to pry. I just want you to be careful. I know you need to protect Emma, but protect yourself too okay. My brother can be...selfish."

I closed my eyes tight and fought back the tears for the first time since Sawyer had returned into my life. Diane's words hit me hard. Diane and Sawyer didn't have the best relationship—they never had—and deep down, I knew her warning came from a place of protection. I think that was one of the major reasons why I'd never told her about us to begin with, because she would have swayed me away from him. It hurt me not to tell her because there wasn't much in our lives that we didn't or hadn't shared with one another. He was the first man in my life, since…well, since himself, and the hurt from before was still there, and I knew that at any time the scab could be ripped off to expose the old wound.

"Brielle, please," she said, coming up behind me and wrapping her arms around me.

"Don't worry, I'll be careful."

9

SAWYER

I LOOKED at my reflection in the mirror, then picked up the bottle of cologne. Tonight Brie and I were going alone on our first official date as a couple. I'd arranged to have my parents watch Emma for the night.

Everything had been crazy over the past week. Diane had found out about us. We then told Brie's mother. Brie had stood up to her, telling her she'd made up the story and that I knew nothing of Emma. She didn't take the news all that well and the look she gave me was one of death. My parents, on the other, hand were ecstatic. Emma was their first grandchild and they snatched the opportunity to have their newfound granddaughter for the night.

I quickly straightened up the living room, just in

case Brie decided to return with me for the night. I'd hope she would. I wanted us to be able to move our history behind us and move on to bigger and better things. I could still feel that connection we'd had when we were younger, and I knew that if given the chance, we had the possibility of being great.

I quickly straightened up the pile of papers and mail on the kitchen table, setting them in one neat pile off to the side. Then I made my way to pick up Brie from The Cooling Rack.

I pulled the car up to the front door and she stepped out and quickly locked the door behind her. The burgundy dress she wore hugged every curve of her body, and I felt my dick twitch as my eyes traced every curve of her body.

"Hey. Sorry about that," she said as she climbed into my car.

"About what?"

"Having to close up. Brenda called in."

"Brie, it's fine. I dropped Emma at my parents' earlier this afternoon and stayed with her until she was comfortable."

"Thank you. I hope she will be okay," Brie said, a look of worry on her face.

"I think she will be just fine. When I left, they were sitting down to have a little ice cream."

Brie nodded. "Should we call and check on her?"

I reached over and took her hand in mine. "Mom and Dad have my number. They said they would call if they needed anything. Tonight I just want us to focus on us."

She softly smiled and nodded, slipping her hand into mine.

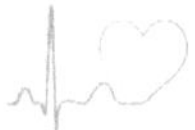

"I HAVEN'T BEEN HERE IN AGES." BRIE LOOKED AROUND at the dining room of her favorite Italian restaurant in all of Eastport—The Lantern House.

"I wonder if they still have your favorite dish?" I said, opening the menu that was in front of me.

She quickly opened hers and perused the menu, looking for her favorite lobster ravioli. She ran over the menu again, slower this time, only to look up at me with a defeated face. "They must have gotten rid of it." She pouted.

"I think you and my sister lived here when you were in your late teens. They probably stopped carrying it after you stopped ordering." I winked.

"Yeah, you are probably right." She giggled.

Brie went back to the menu just as I glanced up

and saw the server standing behind Brie just like we had planned, and I gave a soft nod. He reached around her and placed a bowl down in front of her and smiled. "Your lobster ravioli, miss."

Brie jumped and then looked at me, her eyes bright, and smiled. "How did you do this?"

"I pulled a few strings. The chef is a personal friend of mine."

"Go right ahead, miss," he said, handing her a fork.

I watched as she picked up her fork and dug into the dish, placing piece of ravioli in her mouth and closing her eyes.

"Oh my, Sawyer, it's delicious. Exactly how I remember it," she said, wiping her mouth with her napkin.

I couldn't help but smile as she polished off the bowl while we waited for our main course.

The dishes had just been cleared away, and I had just poured us each another glass of wine and smiled gently at Brie.

"What's on your mind?" she questioned.

"Just thinking about how stupid I was not to tell you how I felt all those years ago." I swallowed hard. I didn't normally talk about my feelings, but I knew this was something she needed to know.

"It's okay, Sawyer. You weren't the only one who was wrong."

"I know, Brie, but I want you to know I am serious. Emma means the world to me and you, while I still feel the same way about you that I did before. These past few months have shown me that. I want to give us another go. A real relationship, not what we were before."

1 0

———

BRIELLE

I SAT THERE, torn between wanting to say yes, and guarding my heart. The look in his eyes told me he was serious, and the undeniable ache I felt in my chest told me to go for it. Now, if any, was the time to trust him.

I was about to answer him when the bill was placed on the table, and Sawyer quickly inserted his credit card into the slip and turned back to me.

"Say something."

As much as I knew protecting us was important, if I didn't begin to trust him with something, there was a chance I never would.

I looked down at my hands and remembered how I felt every single time we'd been together over the past few months. I'd been happy, for the first time in a long time. I could see how much he loved Emma. He never said he was too busy to say good night when she'd cry, he spent most of his days and nights off with us. He'd gone with me when I went to tell my mother, and he stood there and took the heat from her and he defended me when she turned on me for lying to her. He was totally invested, I was sure. "I want that too," I whispered, my insides shaking.

We left the restaurant and were halfway across the parking lot to his car when I reached for his hand. He stopped and turned to look at me. "How long did you ask your parents to keep Emma?" I questioned.

Sawyer turned to me. "They offered to keep her overnight."

"Hmm. I was just thinking that if we are to give us another try, perhaps spending the night alone would be a good idea," I whispered shyly, looking at him.

He placed a hand on my cheek, coming in for a deep kiss. His lips danced over mine in that parking lot. Instantly, my center started to ache, and as soon as he gathered me in his arms, I knew I wanted more.

"Come, let's go," he whispered, pulling me into him as he guided me to his car.

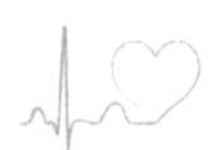

I STOOD IN HIS KITCHEN, MAKING A LATE-NIGHT SNACK for us. Soft music poured through the living room speakers, and I took a sip of wine as I listened to him speak with his mother. I added a few crackers to the plate, and then grabbed a bunch of grapes and added them as well, just as Sawyer stepped into the doorway of the kitchen.

"Any problems?" I asked, focusing on the task at hand.

"She went down no problem. Mom and Dad have no problem keeping her the night. They are thrilled."

I gently swayed to the music as I picked my glass up off the counter and took another sip.

I'd just set the glass down when I felt Sawyer step behind me. The warmth of his skin and scent of cologne enveloped me.

"You almost finished?" he asked, his breath tickling my ear as he brought his hands around and rested them on my abdomen.

I froze at his soft touch. My body was on fire as he pulled me into him. I could feel his hardened cock pressing into my ass as he gently swayed us to the music that played. "You look amazingly sexy in my T-shirt, you know that. That cute ass of yours swaying to the music is going to be my undoing," he whispered.

I closed my eyes and leaned my head against his chest as he brought his lips to the side of my neck. He kissed, at first, and then nibbled as he brought his hands up to cup my breasts. I reached behind me and fisted his shirt as he ran his fingers over my nipples and sucked on the lobe of my ear.

"I think I'm falling in love with you," he whispered into my ear.

I closed my eyes and allowed myself to succumb to him. I, too, felt what he was feeling, only a huge part of me was still afraid to say it. I felt his fingers graze my hips as he lifted his shirt up and over my head. He grabbed and pulled me against his hot skin. I turned my head and met his lips. My skin pebbled as his hand travelled down and slipped inside my panties, running his fingers through my already soaked center.

I reached behind me and palmed his hard cock through his pants.

"Come with me," he whispered.

I turned to follow him and was surprised when he picked me up in his arms. He carried me through the living room and into his bedroom, placing me gently on the bed.

He stood before me, looking down at me, then grabbed my panties and slipped them down my legs. He licked his lips as he took me in, his hand going to the button on his pants. I watched as his fingers flicked it open. He allowed his pants to drop to the floor, and then he dropped his boxers, his cock springing free.

I swallowed hard as he took himself in his hand and began to stroke himself.

"Rub yourself," he whispered breathlessly.

I felt heat surge through my body at his request as I lay there watching his hand form a steady rhythm as he jerked his cock. I closed my eyes and reached down between my legs, sliding my fingers between my lips.

"Fuck, Brie...you're fucking gorgeous," he whispered.

I opened my eyes and looked down at his hand gripping his cock. Sawyer stood there, his impressive cock in his hand with his head cocked back, every muscle in his body tensed, and I could see a bead of precum forming at the tip. I sat up and scooted to the end of the bed, keeping my eyes on him. I didn't touch him. I leaned forward and licked the tip of his cock and then placed my lips around the head. He dropped his cock and brought his hands to the back of my head, lacing his fingers through my hair as I took him completely in my mouth, all the way to the back of my throat.

"Fuck, Brie, slow down," he hissed.

I held onto the base of his cock and let him slide in and out of my mouth a few times before he pushed me back. I dropped his cock as he knelt on the bed and laced his arms underneath my knees. He leaned down and kissed me hard, taking my hand and placing it between my legs.

I knew what he wanted, and I rubbed my clit slowly for him while he reached into the nightstand drawer and pulled out a condom. Our eyes locked as he slid the condom over his cock. I felt him at my opening, slowly pushing at first, and then finally he slid all the way in. I gripped his arms as he pumped into me, kissing me as he went.

I could already feel my climax building and could feel myself tightening around him when he pulled out. He rolled onto his back, breathing heavy.

"Is something wrong?" I questioned.

He bit his lower lip and shook his head. "Get on."

I'd forgotten how Sawyer was: his sexual appetite was insatiable. That, and he loved to change positions. I glanced to his cock and shook my head no. This position was always my undoing, and he knew it.

He rolled over and gently kissed me, placing his hands on my waist he gently coaxed me to straddle his lap. I felt him position himself at my opening, and then with both hands on my hips, he slowly guided me as I lowered onto him. I let out a loud moan as his cock filled me, and I held back my orgasm while I allowed myself to adjust to him.

He gripped my hips and looked up at me. "Rub your clit."

I could tell by the gruffness of his voice that it was more of a command than an request. I slowly began to rock my hips, and I brought my fingers between my legs, slowly rubbing my clit as Sawyer lay against the pillows and watched.

I dropped my head back. I could feel my orgasm building as Sawyer pumped up into me. I leaned forward, and he took my breast in his mouth, gently teasing my nipple with his tongue and teeth. One more time, he ran his teeth gently over the sensitive bud, and I clenched tightly as my orgasm took over my body. I gripped the pillows behind his head as he wrapped his arms around me, pumping up into me until I felt the throbbing of his release.

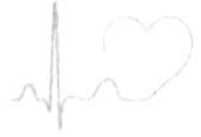

I STARED AT THE GREEN LIGHTS OF HIS ALARM CLOCK. It was only three thirty. I looked over my shoulder to see Sawyer sound asleep. I gently kicked the covers off and slipped his robe on, making my way to the door. I made my way to the washroom, and then made my way into the kitchen to get a drink.

The food still sat on a plate on the counter where we had left it. I grabbed a grape and shoved one into my mouth. As I stood there, my mind quickly ran back to his seduction in the kitchen. I smiled at the thought as my center began to throb again. I blew out a breath and filled a glass with water and sat down at the kitchen table.

I clenched as I sat down. My body hurt. I took a sip of water, thinking back to earlier. I couldn't help but feel the familiar ache between my legs start again as I thought back to last time we'd had sex tonight. It had been different than any other time; this time there was more feeling behind it. It was slower and more sensual. For the first time ever, the man had made love to me.

I blew out a breath. I needed to clear my mind before I went back and crawled into bed. I reached for the grocery fliers that sat in a pile on the table and quietly looked through each one. I was just about to put them all back when a letter addressed to Sawyer caught my eye.

I got up from the chair and looked around the corner toward the bedroom. The light was still off, and I could hear Sawyer gently snoring. I went back and sat down, picking up the letter. It was from a hospital in Florida.

I flipped the page and read the first line, a frown coming to my face the further I read. I flipped the page. It looked like a compensation package. I flipped back to the letter, looking at the date. It was dated a month ago. I flipped through the pages, finally coming to the last page. They needed an answer by next week.

My stomach flipped as I stared down at the papers in front of me. Then, out of the corner of my eye, I caught glimpse of a half-written letter in Sawyer's handwriting. It was addressed to the same hospital. I read what he had written and dropped the letter to the floor. He was taking the job. He'd not mentioned a single word to me about it.

My heart sank and my stomach turned as a flood of panic and hurt filled me, finally turning to anger. Tears filled my eyes as I stared at the letter, finally throwing it down on the table. He'd worked his way in to our little bubble, and now he was leaving. He'd lied about everything.

SAWYER

I woke just as the sun began to peek through the blinds. I stretched, reaching for Brie, only to find her side of the bed cold and empty. I frowned and lifted my head, looking around the bedroom and listening hard. The apartment was silent. I kicked the covers off, slipped into my shorts, and made my way into the living room.

Brie sat on the couch staring off into space, ignoring the fact I had even walked into the room. "There you are," I said, smiling, making my way over to her. I leaned down to kiss her lips, but she turned her face away from me. I frowned. After last night, this wasn't exactly how I imagined this morning going.

"Here I am," she whispered, still not looking at me.

The silence was deafening as I looked down at her emotionless expression.

"Did you sleep okay?"

She shrugged. "As well as I could," she muttered. Her chest rose as she took in a deep breath.

"Would you like some breakfast? I can make you whatever you'd like, bacon, eggs, pancakes, waffles, eggs benedict. You just name it and I'll whip it up," I said, clapping my hands together, a worried feeling coming over me that something was very wrong.

Brie shook her head. "I'm not hungry. Besides, I need to get Emma. Brenda is sick again, which means I have to be at work."

I looked around the room. "Oh, well, why didn't you say so. No need to be stressed. I'll take you to work, and then I'll pick Emma up, take her to the park, and then bring her to The Cooling Rack this afternoon after you're finished."

Brie still didn't look at me. "No, we have time to go get her now," she muttered, getting up from the couch and stepping away from me.

I didn't know what to say. I stood up and looked around the living room and then glanced at my watch. "Emma will have more fun with me than waiting for you at work. That way she won't be underfoot," I said, moving in behind her and running my hands over her chilled arms.

"I said it's fine. I'm used to her being underfoot." She ripped herself away from me, moving over to where her shoes lay on the floor. She slipped her feet in.

I wasn't sure how to respond. She stood there with her back to me. "Brie, is everything okay?"

"I said everything is fine. We have to go."

She stood there sifting through the contents of her purse, her body tense. I didn't have a clue what the problem was. I blew out a breath and then made my way into the bedroom and got dressed.

We drove in silence to my parents' and then to The Cooling Rack. Brie sat beside me staring out the window, while Emma sat in the back of the car chattering away to herself.

I pulled up to The Cooling Rack and parked the car, shutting off the engine, and looked over at Brie. She reached for the handle of the door and climbed out of the car, not once saying anything. She opened the back door and unbuckled Emma, taking her from the seat, then grabbed her overnight bag and shut the door, not saying so much as a word.

I climbed out of the car and walked around to the sidewalk where Brie struggled with both Emma and the bag. I went to grab the overnight bag from her, but she pulled it away. "I'm fine, Sawyer," she bit out. "I've done this alone for years. I've got it."

I held my hands out in front of me. "I was only trying to help."

"And I've told you I don't need your help."

Her eyes said it all: she was angry, and I didn't want to provoke her any more out in the street. Whatever was bothering her would surely come to the surface sooner or later.

"All right, well, call me when you're ready to head home. I'll come and pick you guys up." I could hear the defeat in my voice.

"No need."

"No need? Brie, you don't have your car. You live over fifteen mins away by car. It will take you an hour to walk home, not to mention you don't have Emma's stroller either."

"I said there is no need. I'll have one of the girls take us home."

Brie went to take a couple of steps forward when Emma let out a cry. "Daddy...I want Daddy." She held her little arms out, reaching out for me, tears streaming down her cheeks, but Brie ignored her pleas, still heading for the front door.

"I'll see you later tonight. I'll bring dinner and help put Emma to bed."

Brie stopped walking, turned and looked at me. "Don't feel like you need to come by, Sawyer. Actually, I'd prefer it if you didn't." I caught a glimpse of tears in her eyes as she turned back around, only this time she didn't look back. Instead, she moved forward and pulled the door open, while Emma screamed, still reaching out for me, tears streaming down her face.

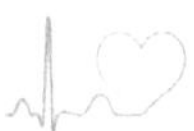

"WHAT THE HELL DID YOU DO?" DIANE SCREAMED INTO the phone.

"What are you talking about?" I asked, getting up off my couch and making my way to the kitchen to grab another slice of pizza.

"Brie called me. She was in tears, mumbling something about how I'd been right. What did you do?" my sister questioned.

I could imagine her standing in front of me, looking at me with a look of death.

"Diane, I didn't do anything. I woke up this morning and she was acting weird." I grabbed a coke out of the fridge, cracking the tab on the can and drinking down the cold liquid.

"You had to have done something. She's a freaking mess. When she called me this morning, she begged me to come pick her up and take her home. I had to leave work. Martha took over my patients. Reggie was pissed, we were so busy."

"What did she say?"

"She wouldn't talk to me. She just said things were over between the two of you. She refused to tell me why, and then said she didn't want to talk about you anymore. So I want to know what it was that you did."

I leaned against the counter and looked down at my feet. I had no idea what had happened. When we'd gone to bed last night, everything was more than fine. I sat down at the kitchen table and put my head in my hands.

"I don't know. We had dinner last night, she spent the night, everything was fine. Emma stayed with Mom and Dad. This morning she was…well, you saw it."

"Sawyer, whatever you've done, you better fix it. That's all I'm going to say. You can't hurt them like this."

"Just wait a minute here. I haven't done anything and I would never hurt either of them. If I knew what the hell I'd done wrong, I would fix it."

"Figure it out! I've got to go."

She didn't even let me say good-bye; she was gone. I needed to get out of here. I needed to clear my head. I stood up, anger coursing through my body but accidentally knocked the pile of papers onto the floor. "Fuck!" I shouted as the papers fell to the floor scattering everywhere.

I bent down and gathered up the papers, placing

them on the table. When I stood up and looked down, it hit me. There, staring up at me, was the offer and letter I'd begun to write to the hospital in Florida. My stomach flopped. Brie had seen it and thought I was accepting the position.

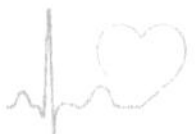

FIVE DAYS LATER

I moved about the halls of the emergency room almost as if in a trance. Sleep hadn't been my friend this past week. I had spent most waking hours trying to get Brie to answer her phone. I'd even gone by The Cooling Rack on my break in hopes she would be there.

"Brenda, I know she is here. Please, you need to get her for me," I'd pleaded.

Brenda just looked at me with pity in her eyes. "I'm sorry, Sawyer, she isn't here. What can I get for you?"

"A coffee," I huffed. "Fine when will she be in?"

"I don't know," Brenda said, setting the coffee I'd ordered in front of me.

"Come on, please. You have to know where she is."

"I'm sorry, I have a line and it's getting longer by the second," she said, barely looking in my direction.

"Can you just leave her a message for me?"

"Fine, here, write it down," she mumbled, ripping a piece of paper off her notepad and placing it on the counter in front of me. "I'll leave her the message okay." She called the person behind me to the counter, pretending to forget I was still standing there.

I scribbled down the note and then headed out the door. I'd done that exact same thing three times this week with the exact same result. I now sat behind the main desk, going over some reports, doing my best to concentrate.

"Earth to Sawyer?"

"Hmmm???" I looked up to see Diane standing beside me holding a few lab reports.

"These are for you. I told you three times they were here."

"Oh, sorry, I was concentrating," I said, taking the papers from her, going right back to the paperwork I was working on.

"You okay?"

"Yep, fine. I've got to go. I need to consult Dr. Richards on a case."

I got up from the desk, knowing full well Diane was watching my every move, and I made my way down the hall to Dr. Richards' office. I stood outside and took a deep breath before knocking on the door.

"Come in."

"Hey, Ryan, do you have a minute?" I asked, stepping inside.

"Hey, yes, come on in. Please take a seat. So have you made your decision?"

I took a seat and nodded. "I have."

"And?"

"And I am going to have to turn it down. I've already written to them."

Ryan looked at me, a little perplexed at my decision. After all, I had shared with him my intentions to advance my career when I had first arrived. "Oh, have you changed your mind about advancing?"

I shook my head. "No, I haven't. I would just prefer to advance my career here."

"Sawyer, you can tell me to mind my own business, but I am curious about the change in your decision," Ryan said, sitting back against his chair. "I figured I would only have you for a little while especially with your goals."

I blew out a breath. "There's been a change in my personal life, and right now I need to stay put."

Ryan flipped his pencil between his fingers and looked at me. "Is everything okay?"

"I'm a father," I bit out.

I swallowed hard, praying I would be able to get Brie to talk to me again so I could be a father to Emma.

Ryan looked at me, a smile coming to his face. "Congratulations, my friend. We are definitely going to have to celebrate at some point. So I guess that means you will be joining us at the Christmas party this year?"

"I will." I smiled.

"I'm somewhat relieved, to be honest. I didn't want to have to hire someone again," Ryan said as I stood up.

I'd just gotten to the door when my name was paged. "Guess I have to go," I said, opening the door.

"Have a good day, Sawyer."

1 2

SAWYER

One week Later

EMMA SAT at the kitchen table eating Cheerios while I loaded up my bag with snacks for her. It was almost six. I'd been late to work almost every day this past week. Emma hadn't been sleeping. All she did was cry for Sawyer, and my nerves were shot. I'd spent every night tossing and turning.

I popped a couple boxes of juice into my bag as Emma looked up at me. "Baby, why don't you eat?" I asked and jumped when the phone rang.

Emma looked up at me from where she sat. "Daddy?" she questioned as she brought her hands up and rubbed her tired eyes and began to cry.

I turned to the phone, looking at the display, and closed my eyes. It was Sawyer, all right, calling from the hospital once again. I blew out a breath and went back to packing my bag.

"Daddy, Daddy..." Emma chanted.

It was like she knew it was him. As I stood there listening to her, a tear slipped down my cheek. It was best to just let him float on out of our lives, I thought to myself. It would be easier that way. If I were able to do that, I knew that Emma would eventually forget him—or so I hoped. I, on the other hand, would have a harder time getting over him.

"Eat your breakfast, sweetie," I said, wiping the tear from my cheek and placing my hand on her head and smoothing her hair. "We have to go soon."

Emma sat there and cried, then picked up the small plastic bowl of Cheerios and dumped it onto the kitchen floor. I looked down at the mess, tears filling my eyes, and grabbed the broom, sweeping them into a little pile as Emma screamed.

The Cooling Rack was already busy by the time we arrived. My patience was on the short side, and I was happy that when I put Emma down in my office with her toys she began playing with them instead of crying.

Exhausted and feeling sick to my stomach, I began my day, prepping sheets of cookies and croissants to proof then decorating cakes and cupcakes. It was a little after eight when the door to the kitchen opened and Diane popped her head in.

"Morning," she called, a soft smile falling on her lips.

"Hey."

"You have a minute?"

"Not really," I said with a defeated sigh, looking around at all the orders I still had left to bake and box.

"You look exhausted. You're coming to sit down," Diane said, taking one hard look at me.

I didn't know who I was trying to fool. Anyone who took one look at me would see the exact same thing. When I didn't move, she came over, took my shoulders, and guided me into my office. I plopped down on a chair and looked up at her.

"What?" I asked.

"Have you eaten this morning?"

I shook my head. I hadn't eaten dinner last night either because by the time I'd finally gotten Emma to sleep, my head ached so badly I knew food would only make me sick.

"Brenda," Diane called, "could you bring us two coffees and a couple croissants please." Diane looked down at me. Brenda appeared at the door in seconds with everything Diane had asked for.

"Would you mind taking Emma for a second?" she questioned.

"Of course. Come on, munchkin," Brenda said, holding her hand out to Emma. "Let's go outside for a moment."

As soon as they were gone, Diane closed the door and sat down beside me. "Now what happened?"

I looked at her, refusing to break down, even though every fiber of my body was screaming just to cry and get it over with. "You were right."

"About..."

"About your brother being a selfish prick. I should have known better."

"I never said he was a selfish prick. I simply said he could be selfish. Now what happened?"

"I found a job offer in his kitchen from a hospital down in Florida. Did you know he applied? He promised me he was here for good, yet here he is applying for positions that take him away. I also found the beginnings of a letter saying he was accepting the job." I placed my face in my hands and drew in a deep breath. "I never should have let him in. I certainly shouldn't have let him into Emma's life. I curse the day I ever laid eyes on him."

"Whoa, now just a minute. Don't you do that. If

you hadn't of met him, then you wouldn't have Emma."

I got up out of the chair I was sitting in and paced back and forth. "I know, I just..."

"Brielle, I know for a fact that Sawyer turned down that job offer."

"How do you know that?"

"Brielle, things spread like wildfire through that hospital. He didn't even apply for it. The hospital submitted a recommendation on his behalf because he shows so much promise to move up and there were no positions open here."

I blew out a breath and looked at my best friend. "I don't know, Diane."

"I do. Look, as much as Sawyer and I don't see eye to eye on things, I can say that he has changed since he found out about Emma. It's almost as if overnight he became a completely different person. Everything he's been doing lately has been for both you and Emma. I saw him at work yesterday. He's an absolute mess. I've actually never seen him this upset and worked up before."

I sat quiet for a moment, letting Diane's words sink into my mind. Sifting through everything she'd said about the job offer he'd received. Then I looked at her. "Did he tell you to come here?"

"Do you think for one second that I would come

here if he asked me to? That I would lie to you for him if what I were saying isn't true?"

Never in my life had Diane ever done anything Sawyer had asked, especially if he were being deceitful. "No, I guess not."

"Exactly. I'm here because I care about you, and I care about my niece. If he makes you happy, then you should be with him. If he doesn't, then that is okay too, but don't throw away something because of something you saw. Especially when you don't have all the information you need to make a proper decision. You need to talk to him."

Just then the door to my office opened. I looked up to see a disheveled looking Sawyer. He looked at both of us before giving me an awkward smile, for the first time he didn't exude the confidence he'd always had. "Can I speak to you?"

Our eyes met and a funny feeling ran through my body as he stood there looking back at me.

"I'm going to run," Diane said, hugging me. She stood up and turned toward the door and stopped, leaning into Sawyer and whispering something before leaving my office.

Sawyer waited until Diane had left and then he took a seat beside me. He took hold of my hand and looked up at me. "We need to talk, Brie."

I looked down at my hand in his and closed my eyes, fighting back more tears.

"I know you saw the offer and the letter."

I nodded and swallowed hard. I was afraid that if I spoke, my voice would crack and give away how hurt I was. I reached over and took a sip of the coffee Diane had gotten for me, and then I looked to Sawyer. "Why didn't you tell me about it?"

"Because there was never anything to tell. I was never going to take that job. I never even applied for it. The letter you saw, I wrote it just to get it out of my system." He squeezed my hand and looked at me. "You know you could have just asked me about it," he whispered.

I looked at him with tear-filled eyes. "It wasn't my place."

"Yes, it is. I told you I wasn't going anywhere. I am fully committed to us, to this family."

"Yeah, but..."

"No, no buts. You and Emma mean everything to me. I swear to you, I'm not going anywhere. I'm in love with you, in love with us, in love with her."

"You are?"

"Yes, Brie, I am. I wasted a chance with you once. I'm not doing it again. I'm not going to throw away another chance with you."

I looked at him, unsure of what he was talking

about. I figured what he had said to me when we first got together was just to get me to speak with him again. I didn't think his feelings were real. "Sawyer, please, I don't think you were ever in love with me."

"I was so in love with you I didn't date for almost two years. I'm head over heels in love with you." Sawyer leaned in and placed his hand on my cheek, wiping away the tear that had strayed from my eye with his thumb. He leaned forward and placed a kiss on my lips.

As we parted, the door to my office opened, and Brenda walked in with Emma. She was carrying a flower in her little hands. "Here, Mommy..." she said, holding out the flower to me, and then she spotted Sawyer.

The second she laid her eyes on him, she dropped the purple flower and brought her little hands up to her mouth in surprise. "Daddy!" she screamed, stomping her little legs in excitement.

Sawyer took one look at her and scooped her up into his powerful arms, bringing her in for a hug. "Baby girl..." he said, kissing her forehead as she wrapped her arms around his neck. "I missed you."

I stood up and looked around my messy office, then looked out to the mess of the kitchen. I wiped the tears from my eyes, then looked to Sawyer who stood there holding Emma in his arms. I'd missed him so much, and I hadn't been able to fully admit to myself how much he had truly met to me until he hadn't been around.

"I'm sorry, Sawyer."

"Don't be. We just need to get better at communication. Both of us do. It's going to take time, but we will get there."

He reached out and pulled me into him. I placed my head on his shoulder and took in a deep breath, the scent of his cologne filling my nostrils. The feeling of his arms around me put me at complete ease. Just then Brenda walked into the kitchen and signaled to me.

I smiled and popped my head out the door. "What's up?"

"Is Mrs. Benson's order ready yet? She's here to pick it up."

I looked around, feeling completely defeated. The pile of orders was a mile high, and I would never get everything done with Emma underfoot.

"Give me twenty minutes," I said, pushing the hair out of my face, running for the order form.

"Look, why don't I take Emma out of your hair and let you finish up here. When you get home, we can talk, sort things out?" Sawyer said, coming up behind me.

I bit my bottom lip and looked down to where

Emma sat playing with her toys. "Are you sure you don't mind?"

"I'm positive." He leaned in and placed a kiss on my lips. "We'll see you at home."

"See you at home."

13

BRIELLE

Six Month's later

"Pick a hand," Sawyer said, holding both hands out in front of me in a closed fist.

I looked at him and smiled. "What are you up to?"

"Just pick a hand."

Emma looked up from where she sat on the floor with her toys and giggled. "Daddy's being silly isn't he," I said, reaching out and touching his right hand.

He flipped it over and opened his hand to reveal a silver key. I frowned as he held the key out in front of me. "Here you go."

"What is this?" I questioned, still looking at the dangling key he held in front of me.

"This is the key to our new place. The condo we went to look at a month ago is ours."

My jaw dropped and excitement ran through me. We had been discussing moving in together for the past three months. My place was too small for us, and his place was on the other side of town, too far from The Cooling Rack if I needed to walk. We had looked at some places but weren't able to agree on one, until we had seen this condo. Problem was there was a bidding war going on between two other buyers.

"How did you do this? I thought that our agent didn't want to us to get in the middle of it."

Sawyer gave me that cocky smile I loved so much. "When have you ever known me to listen." He winked.

I laughed. "What happened?"

"Well, I couldn't help it. I put in an offer. Of course, both couples raised theirs. I offered again, one dropped out. The other person raised his offer, and I decided to let him have it, but he couldn't get the financing, so it's ours!"

Excitement overtook me. "When do we move?"

"Place closes in sixty days. Get packing, baby!" he said, grabbing me and picking me up off the floor, kissing me hard.

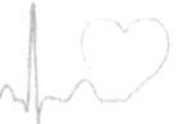

FOUR MONTHS LATER, WE HELD OUR FIRST FAMILY dinner in our dining room. We had a lot to celebrate. Mom had finally forgiven me for lying to her all those years ago, and she had finally accepted Sawyer. Diane had finally finalized her divorce from Leo. She had moved into her new place and had started her new role at the hospital in the Pediatric Intensive Care Unit. Sawyer's parents now took turns with my mother babysitting Emma. Mom would take her the days she went to kindergarten, and his parents would take her the days she didn't. It worked well.

Sawyer and I worked hard on our relationship every day. We were well past the hurt stage, and we had learned to trust one another again. He stayed right where he was, in the emergency department of Eastport General. Emergency was his passion—he loved the fast pace, the challenge, and the fact that every day was different.

The Cooling Rack was finally really booming. Everyday there were more and more orders, and finally I had to hire a second baker, especially when I could no longer keep up with all the other work.

Sawyer would propose to me the following Christmas. It had taken us a long time to get where we finally were, but we were here, and I couldn't be happier.

I'd always had a strong feeling that one day he would be mine, even from the time I had been a teenager. There was no doubt about it, Sawyer would always be my one and only Doctor Desire.

Doctor D's Orderly Affair by CA King
Doctor Trouble by E.M. Shue
Doctor Temptation by Syd Ryan
Dueling Doctors by DC Renee
Doctor Sexy by TL Mayhew
Doctor Fix-It by Mel Walker
Doctor One of a Kind by Anjelica Grace
Doctor Casanova by Emma Nichole
Dirty Doctor by Amanda Richardson
Doctor All Nighter by Adora Crooks
Doctor Desire by S.L. Sterling

A NOTE FROM THE AUTHOR

Dear Readers,

I would like to thank you for taking the time to read *Doctor Desire part of the Doctors of Eastport General Series. I loved writing this story and I hope that you enjoyed Sawyer and Brielle's story as much as I enjoyed writing it.* If you did, I would love it if you would drop me a review. Reviews are so important and really help me; plus I love to hear what my readers think.

Coming Soon
Ace (Book 2 Vegas MMA) May 10, 2022
Blade (Book 3 Vegas MMA) July 8, 2022

You can find all information about Ace and Blade by visiting my website.

ABOUT THE AUTHOR

S.L. Sterling had been an avid reader since she was a child, often found getting lost in books. Today if she isn't writing or plotting, she can be found buried in a romance novel. S.L. Sterling lives with her husband and dog in Northern Ontario.

Prefer to stay in touch by Newsletter:
Sign up here

Visit my
Website

You can also join my Reader Group
Sterlings Silver Sapphires

Constraint